Champagne at Seven!

Bitches of Fifth Avenue
Book One

Books by Toni Glickman

Bitches of Fifth Avenue
Book One: Champagne at Seven!

Coming Soon!
Bitches of Fifth Avenue
Book Two: Cutthroat Couture
Book Three: Designer Deceit

For more information
visit: www.SpeakingVolumes.us

Champagne at Seven!

Bitches of Fifth Avenue
Book One

Toni Glickman

SPEAKING VOLUMES, LLC
NAPLES, FLORIDA
2022

Champagne at Seven!

ISBN 978-1-64540-727-0

To my children, with love.

Acknowledgments

To everyone who helped me get this story onto the page. Notably my family and friends. To the incredible Nancy Rosenfeld! Thank you for your time, feedback, love and support. I want to acknowledge, and express my own personal appreciation for the long and hellish hours I spent, day after day and year over year at the multitude of brands I tirelessly dedicated myself to—without any of these, I wouldn't have had the story I would eventually be inspired to write about.

Chapter One

Dinner on N Street

6:15 p.m.

For the past eight hours, Olivia Wyatt has been in fifth gear high-drama mode, busting her Pilates and yoga toned ass to pull off the impossible. Only now, with forty-five minutes left until the official VIP (Olivia prefers the term *Very Important Prick*) arrival, does she take a final, critical blue-eyed inventory of her frenetically neurotic efforts.

Flowers:

In the foyer, a white hydrangea bouquet decorates the Eaves console on the left; three tight white rose and lily of the valley arrangements adorn the dinner table, evenly centered and positioned exactly ten inches apart in their square, clear glass containers. (Olivia always preferred white flower arrangements. *So fresh looking!*) In the powder room, the aroma of hyacinth drowns out sneaky cigarette smoke—Olivia's no smoking rule never seems to matter late at night when all house rules blur from chardonnay and whiskey overload. *What else . . . what else?* Oh, the gardenia tree next to the black iron doors leading to the garden. A last-minute order, but Potomac Petals always makes the impossible possible! Even the rare Honduran Valley mini orchid in that gorgeous shade of pumpkin orange was no issue for last year's Halloween bash.

Flowers; check!

Dining room . . .

The custom Italian-designed clear acrylic table gleams, while the freshly buffed black and white tiled floor is beautifully obvious from underneath. (Ever since she saw the Mark Hotel lobby in New York City, she just *had to have the same look!*) Under perfectly remote-control dimmed LED lighting, the table settings glisten: simple and round white porcelain plates, sterling Christofle flatware and Baccarat crystal glasses, water and wine, all entirely spotless. (Olivia herself painstakingly buffed out all fingerprint smudges.) Edwin would ask why she would burden herself with such a chore? "Especially since we have staff, Olivia," part of his arrogance Olivia hated. *Pretentious motherfucker!* Olivia pondered. Neighboring the plates are crisp, white Irish linen napkins, each folded origami-style. Olivia originally considered obelisk-shaped, mimicking the Washington Monument, then deemed that phallic and cliché, opting for more intricately sculpted camellia flowers—more *wow* factor and an indirect nod to Coco Chanel, Olivia's icon of all icons. Such small details never fail to impress this crowd.

Table, check!

Now . . . the food . . .

Olivia quickly runs through the menu in her head: *mini crepes with crème fraiche, cut chives and Beluga caviar, zucchini flowers fried in first press Italian olive oil, and parmesan crusted artichoke hearts. Then the main course, and Edwin's favorite; thinly sliced beef tenderloin, mushroom risotto with thinly shaved truffles and flat leaf Italian parsley to decorate and finish the presentation. Always to accompany is a simple green salad—dressed simply with fresh lemon juice, EVOO, and a generous dash of salt and freshly ground black pepper. Finally, affogato, the drink-dessert, satisfying both an after-dinner coffee and pining for something sweet desire. As an alternative, there is the luscious black forest cake, just in case some high-maintenance sugar addict is in demand of something more decadent.*

Claudia, her live-in housekeeper and nanny, (and friend, if Olivia was being honest) spent hours racing around to buy the menu's ingredients, but now, she seems unperturbed, shuffling around in the kitchen. Olivia can hear her, pans clanging as she sings along to Latin heartthrob, Juanes . . . "Y tu puedes decirle a todos, Que esta es tu canción, Y aunque suenen un poco simple Lo que te digo hoy . . .!" She worked for the former Italian Ambassador for years . . . that is, until *the* scandal—*Four Seasons hotel, three escorts, two grams of coke*—you get the picture. In fact, everyone did, as those paparazzi shots made the *Washington Post's Style Section*. (D.C.'s version of NY Post's Page 6.) The very second Maurizio hightailed it back to Roma, Olivia snapped Claudia right up. That was years ago, when Gwynnie, her precious baby girl, and the only good thing that came out of her marriage, was barely out of diapers. Edwin always cracked some sort of obnoxious joke right in front of dear Claudia. "What time are tacos?! Isn't it Tuesday?" followed by that annoying and patronizing laugh of his. "Bwahahahha!!"

Dinner, check!

Wait, I'm forgetting something . . .

Oh, shit! Olivia speed walks to the living room, chest tightening with anxiety. She thinks, *Where the fuck is my inhaler? An asthma attack never fails to hit me when I'm stressed!* Olivia takes a big hit from her Symbicort and slowly exhales as she closes her eyes. Counting back from five, she comes back to reality, (insert deer in the headlights look), and realizes she forgot about the most important thing of all . . . Potomac Liquor was set to deliver, but . . . forget gardenia trees, truffles and goddamn camellia flower shaped napkins . . . without booze, this party is DOA. She could already hear the neighborhood gossip and see the *Georgetowner's* headline. "Wyatt Party Disaster! Has Olivia Lost It? Page 4 has this sizzling story!"

Eying the bar, Olivia sighs with relief. *Phew!* They are fully-stocked—Claudia must have signed for the order. It's all there: vodka, scotch, tequila, vermouth, gin, rum, red and white wine, whisky and ten extra bottles of champagne. Olivia firmly believed there should always be champagne perfectly cooled at 52°F degrees and ready to pour. Despite the local elite's insistence, Olivia firmly believes that Veuve Clicquot is totally overrated. *I love that incredible orange label and all but, truly, I prefer Robert Moncuit . . . it has an underground following . . . less mainstream*—a case always in the wine cellar and six bottles cooling in the wine fridge. A seemingly useless device that becomes a staple, Olivia purchased the Auto-Chill from one of those gadgety, in-flight airline catalogs. (She has no recollection of buying it; probably happened sometime between cocktail number one, and the pre-flight 5mg. Xanax) In fact, without realizing it, her arm is already reaching out . . . *I earned this;* Olivia tells herself.

Olivia prefers a clear head when party prepping, but pops the cork anyway, deeming these *extraordinary circumstances.* She pours the bubbly into a Tiffany champagne flute—a wedding gift . . . *gosh these things have lasted forever,* she thinks—and tells herself it isn't a problem. Sure, she's found herself drinking more as of late, but comparable to what? This is D.C., after all, where alcohol is practically a 6th USDA food group. Libations make the capital go 'round, as they say, and the city has 2,000 AA meetings a week to prove the fact.

Olivia takes a long gulp, body instantly warming, limbs loosening. *Why am I being so negative?* She asks herself, downing half the glass quickly. True, it was inconsiderate of Edwin, throwing this dinner party at her last minute, but there was a time when she would have relished the challenge. Olivia is a gifted hostess—that fact is widely acknowledged. Once, Olivia Wyatt was the new and improved Evangeline Bruce . . . D.C.'s most infamous hostess . . . only younger, sexier and with a way better wardrobe. What would Olivia do without Françoise in the Neiman's designer salon? "Darleeng, zee perfect dresz juzt delivered in zee sztore. You must call me immediate, oui? I'm holding your zize. I juszt know you are going to love eet, oui . . . eet iz you!"

As a newlywed, Olivia threw herself fully into the planning of events, from cocktail parties to full-fledged blow-outs. To her, there were no dinner parties, there were "lifestyle experiences." She'd spend days contemplating every detail, from the menu, to the lighting scheme, to even creating customized soundtracks for each unique occasion . . . sometimes *La Boheme* for peanuts and cocktails, Frank Sinatra for appetizers and Rod Stewart's *Da Ya Think I'm Sexy* just for a little shock factor. She was fearless, always staying true to herself even amongst the vast resources, infinite options, large budgets and guests that often included her husband's associates—men who ranged from charming rogues to snobbish, uptight douchebags. Still, despite the various downtown K Street reputations and plethora of Capitol Hill gossip, she refused to give in to preconceived notions, approaching each guest with an open mind and big, welcoming cashmere-enveloped arms.

It hadn't been an easy transition, acclimating to Edwin's First-Class world, but after all these years, Olivia had finally found a happy medium. Okay, maybe happy was the wrong word, but she fit in well enough, yet hadn't totally surrendered herself to the D.C. ice queen society dark side. She'd never be one of those pinched-lip, judgmental bitches in predictable St. John's tweed knits or the other "Preppy Handbook" lot. Olivia thought of herself as classic with a Pucci punk rock-edge, and could intelligently discuss a range of topics, from environmental issues to Maddow vs. Hannity debates, all while keeping true to herself. Olivia was a woman who laughed loud, dropped the f-bomb and wore a Swarovski crystalized skull and cross bone belt with her cocktail dress. Not pearls. If she ever did pull out her Mikimoto's, she added a chain or two, à la Coco, and her diamond safety pin earrings. Just another way to stay unique in a D.C. fishbowl of matchy-matchy, boring black and navy suits.

She entertained the same way.

For all the exuberant, enthusiastic planning, Olivia would let loose, burst to life and win over even the most difficult of guests . . . without even trying. Her unique charm and wit—her personal secret ingredients—never to be bought nor duplicated, were the real key. These qualities were the reasons why Edwin fell in love with Olivia—her valiant, non-apologetic spark. Just being herself is what made Olivia D.C.'s most interesting and recognized hostess.

Now, more than a decade later, something had changed . . . Olivia had a sneaking suspicion it just might be her. Perhaps it had happened in increments, or in a rush, but there it was, unmistakable. Olivia looks down at her glass, which is more than half-empty, the same way she had begun to view her life. *I used to live for this shit*, she thinks. Once Olivia was the beating fucking heart at the center of every social gathering. She drains the drink, remembering those days.

Champagne at Seven!

A few years into their marriage, they'd hosted a dinner party for Edwin's newest clients and his first politically based campaign. *That had been quite the night*, Olivia thinks to herself. Edwin had been nervous, feeling out of his element—he could win over the most difficult of CEO's, charm the most jaded of high-profile personalities, but the White House crowd? They were a different beast. And even more, these were the conservative set—and not the fun kind, either. On the Pence-Reagan good times 1-10 fun scale, this bunch ranked lower towards the Mike and Karen's snooze level two cookies-and-bible study than to Nancy and Ron's whoopin'-it-up with celebrities on the California ranch level 10 blow-out. With Olivia's help, by the end of the evening, not only was the uptight bunch undeniably trashed, but she had convinced an older, notoriously uptight, Jim Baker look-alike, Brooks Brothers black (*brown before 6:00!*) leather cap-toed Oxford wearing Congressman to play a game of charades.

"You know who you are?" The Congressman had said once the interlude came to an end, his face flushed with pleasure. "The girl in the movie. The one with the gloves and long cigarette . . . you know . . . the Hepburn girl?"

Breakfast at Tiffany's? Olivia had said, delighted.

"Yes, exactly! That's the one. Holly Golightly, that was her name. That's you, Mrs. Wyatt. The Holly Golightly of Georgetown." Then he'd reached for her hand, as gracefully as a young man, gently kissed it and looked into her eyes. The man didn't know that he was talking about something else . . . freedom. Leaning into the present moment. In that split-second, as he smiled and looked into her eyes, she saw the sparkle of who he'd once been, long ago. Before his time in the Nixon administration, or at the golf outings with Bush One and Bush Two; before long days of babble in the halls of Washington and tedious lunches at The Palm on 19th Street. In the tiny flicker of a moment, she saw the decades younger man, the rowdy, rabble-rousing-Exeter-Yalie who charmed every co-ed in his wake.

What happened to me? thinks Olivia, refilling her flute. She glances up, catching sight of herself in the bar mirror. She narrows her eyes, taking in her tight navy sheath with skyscraper high front slit, wide, black leather laser-cut, Alaia belt, and Repetto Cendrillon black ballet flats. With her 5'9" stature and inherent conviction, Louboutins weren't necessary. Time for the final and most important accent—she crosses to the table, finds her Chanel clutch and reaches inside. Back to the mirror, she uncaps the tube, twists and then slowly, with painstaking care, applies a coat of her favorite armor of all time. Pink lipstick, her signature. An Elsa Peretti sterling silver Bone cuff on her right wrist anchored the look.

The final step before any occasion, it fills her with a surge of confidence, adding that last touch before stepping into that world. Edwin's world. Tonight, a subtle peony pink, but whether sunset blush or magnetic magenta, it feels like protection against the world, adding that final boost of attitude and honorary *don't fuck with me* silent shout out. The shade changed alongside her mood. And, sometimes, a shade even changed her mood. *There.* Olivia takes a step back and scrutinizes the final product. She looks elegant and polished. Hair, makeup, nails, skin, dress, shoes and her most favorite accessory; pink lipstick.

A wry chuckle. Olivia toasts her reflection.

Olivia dressed by instinct. In fact, she relied on instinct to steer her through life—on nights like this, outfit selection was critical. She would stand in her closet and look around. Slowly. Look and think—and wait to feel something. An inspiration from even one item; maybe a novel or seasonal piece . . . maybe a skirt, top, a jacket. She'd build her look, item by item, always by instinct, and knew what worked and what didn't. Often enough, she would go to her accessories first. Jewelry, watches, bangles, shoes, belts, scarves, bags, necklaces, earrings. One item would dictate which one would come next.

Olivia could never quite understand why some of her friends just couldn't put a plain white V-neck tee-shirt and a simple pair of plain blue jeans together. For them it was tortured misery to think about the challenge. To Olivia, it was fun. A game even. A time to color in her own unique canvas to show the world who she was.

Olivia quickly came back to reality and remembered why she even got dressed for the evening. She took another sip of champagne and refocused on her immediate to-do list.

If there were an Olympic category for faking it, Olivia would bring home the gold. She would plaster on a big smile, keep up a steady stream of small talk, and ask the right leading questions. And nod. A lot. She'd compliment the merry-go-round of Very Important Pricks, while secretly thinking the majority were narcissistic man-boys who equated their bloated portfolios to personal charisma. As for the women, they seemed a rotating cast of dried-up housewives and DAR matriarchs. And then, of course, there were also the botoxed, bleached out second housewives and secret inside the beltway wannabes obsessed with certain choice D.C. zip codes.

That was D.C.—reputation defined by the names you drop, where you work and where you went to school. And, maybe, the most important of all, were the numbers in your cell phone. It was all about image, and the Wyatt name could take you far. Smile and nod. Smile and nod. Ask a question here and there, look impressed. Throw out a reference—a name they might know, an exclusive event—to show you are on an equal playing field. Smile and nod some more. *Et voila!* You are officially someone worth knowing.

For the past several years, it had been the complete opposite. She'd done everything possible to avoid hosting even the smallest event. She faked being sick, faked girlfriend emergency dramas, a colonoscopy in the morning. An allergy attack or bad hair day. Any legit sounding justification.

She had officially entered the *I really don't give a crap about any of this pointless horseshit anymore,* zone. Olivia paced and circled, inside her own home, waiting for the first guest to arrive.

Chapter Two

Running from Nothing

The day had started out like any other. Olivia had a packed agenda. A busy day helped her stay focused on anything else but the misery she had at home with *Operation Keep Edwin Occupied.* God forbid he was ever bored. Olivia made sure there was always something on the calendar, just so she didn't have to hear his chronic complaining about having nothing to do just after opening the front door at 6:00 p.m. "Why are you always home so early? No professional working Washingtonian human being ever gets home before 8:00." She pestered. "Listen," Edwin said. "I'm the boss. I can do whatever the hell I want." She rolled her eyes and checked the texts on her iPhone.

Type A, obsessive, hyper-focused. She was all of them, and her personal daily routine was a part of her . . . like breathing. It helped keep her somewhat centered and focused in a D.C. agenda-driven world of superficial bullshit. The flippant upkeep was as necessary as the cream in her coffee.

Her daily schedule:

Morning. 6:00 alarm. Brush teeth, (another Xanaxed/drunk airplane purchase yielded that $900 Samsung electric three speed toothbrush-water flosser) and gargle with fresh mint Listerine. Grab the white terry monogrammed robe, stumble downstairs, and shove an environmentally friendly pod of 365 Organic French Roast in the Brew Master 5000, add a healthy "splash" of organic half and half, and drink two thirds . . . the second cup warm up . . . always from her favorite iris blue ceramic mug she bought that one summer while on vacation in Antibes. Provence is beautiful, sure. She still preferred Paris.

Next, skincare and her favorite part of the a.m. daily routine:

Hair in a ponytail, snap on a white cotton headband—mandatory to maintaining blow-dry longevity—and begin initial cleansing. Something mild for the morning—a light geranium infused cleansing oil, most likely—then pat dry and do skin intake via the 15x lighted magnification mirror (yes, another inflight Xanax Sky Mall purchase). Never a pleasant task, but a necessary one. Dry? Oily? Unexpected spots or blemishes? Or, horror of horrors, one of her infrequent stress induced rosacea outbreaks? If so, she'd make a mental note and call the dermatologist. Extra haggard or the beginnings of a new crease? Mental note, part deux: *Dr. Alster emergency 911 Botox appointment!*

That day, there had been no dermatologic emergencies. Skin diagnosis: Normal. Perfectly hydrated and even luminous. Editorial worthy, some might say. *Your complexion is so beautiful*, women had often told her over the years. *What's your secret?* The correct answer: *Oh, you're so silly!* (insert waving off a compliment hand gesture) *I'm a mess!* The reality: regularly scheduled 90-minute facial appointments, good genes, and expensive, no, make that very expensive products . . . ranging from glycolic-based to papaya-infused. Japanese Matcha tea cleansing powders, French lavender and English jasmine balms, bamboo and brown rice concocted concentrated exfoliants. Endless and miscellaneous serums, anti-aging hyaluronic acid injected Japanese cotton squares. Nutrient packed eye creams, designer SPFs, emollience creams and Hungarian rosehip and pomegranate moisture mists. Even down to her go-to Sara Happ lip scrub and balm. *That one-time impulse add-on at Blue Mercury became a total obsession!* And most important of all? Her massive collection of masks. Hydrating, brightening, exfoliating, conditioning, vitamin-C, clay, collagen and clarifying just to name a few. Her new favorite being the Hanacure, All-In-One facial mask.

Next, a quick spray of dry shampoo and brush through of yesterday's blow-out, followed by a light makeup application; Lancome Defencils black mascara, Chanel Beige face powder & Sisley Phyto lip-twist tinted balm in #6 Cherry. Finally, outfit selection. Usually, tight-fitting L'Agence "Marguerite" dark indigo skinny jeans, paired with a retro graphic tee and Isabel Marant black leather jacket. Golden Goose metallic and glitter-superstar sneakers finished her daytime look.

Next, her daughter Gwynnie's wake-up call:

Wake-ups were always a gamble, ranging from a sleepy-eyed "Hi Mommy! You look so pretty!" to sheet-over-head moaning and groaning. Equally unpredictable would be the following hour, which might consist of her bubbly, affectionate babble, or eye-rolling complaints as to why there was no Raisin Bran, her favorite go-to breakfast, paired with whatever plant "milk" was trending.

That morning had been, "Diet flakes with freeze dried strawberries? For reals? And still no Raisin Bran? What's the dealio?" She'd said, looking at the Special K box. When Olivia explained she'd just been changing it up, Gwynnie had sighed. "Mom, fruit grows on trees. Freeze drying is the devil's work. Preservatives, weird chemicals . . . I read a whole article on it in health class.

Raisins are at least a socially acceptable dried fruit. WTF!"

Olivia had made a mental note: *grocery store. Or better yet, Amazon Prime.*

Whatever the state of Gwynnie's hormones, Olivia relished those morning moments alone with her child. Her private girl's school was highly prestigious—she mingled with the daughters of Ambassadors, journalists, CEO's and hedge funders—and the curriculum was particularly demanding. Between the excessive homework and extracurricular activities, there was never much mother-daughter time, so Olivia grabbed every second she could.

7:30 a.m. Departure for school:

Olivia would pull up to the curb and offer last minute reminders. "Don't forget the check for the field hockey uniform . . . return the library books . . ." then tell her daughter she loved her. As for Gwynnie, her response varied . . . like her morning wake up . . . either returning the sentiment or giving a halfhearted, "me too." And right on cue, Olivia rolled the window down, smiled and yelled out a loud "I LOVE YOU!" while ignoring the signals of the orange-vested wearing carpool Nazis. She quietly, and always, swore them off in her head; *you annoying sacks of shit!*

Barely fifteen and already 5'8", her long-limbed off-spring was far from the pimply and gangly teenage stereotype. Backpack slung over shoulder, her pleated navy skirt looking more choice than uniform, Olivia had watched her daughter's lithe figure, beautiful face and perfect skin, slice through the dewy morning grass, friends falling in step at her sides. Her confidence was obvious as her Adidas Sambas sashayed their way across The Oval at the center of campus. Without fail, Olivia felt that rush of unconditional love and stunned bewilderment. Gwendolyn moved through the world like someone who knew exactly where she was headed.

8:25 a.m. With morning daughter drop off complete, Olivia would officially launch into her scheduled appointments, tasks and self-created obligations. First, a quick Starbucks (tall dark roast, extra cream and one Splenda), then, come 8:55, her first appointment: Copenhaver . . . *the* Washington go-to stationery destination—*God, I hope there's parking*, Olivia had thought. She had a deadline and needed to peruse cardstock options, come to a decision and put in the order. Invites for the upcoming charity gala had to be finished and sent out by the following Monday at the latest. Because she was such a regular, the store was opening early, just for her.

The task was not one she looked forward to, but this was part of her job as a member of the *WTC*, or Women's Thrive Collective. *More like WTF*, Olivia thought to herself, as she often did. While an active member, she wasn't exactly a proud one.

A noted D.C. based philanthropic 501(c)(3) organization; the *WTC* hosted regular fundraisers. That day's invites were for their upcoming . . . *shit, what was it?* While parked, Olivia guiltily checked the Collective's most recent email on her phone. *Oh, yes. To help kids who preferred Sour Patch Kids and Smarties move to healthier fruit and vegetable snack options*. Though, in official *WTC* speak, they would *be fundraising to support the nutritional education of D.C.'s less-fortunate youth.* Either way, it sounded like a joke.

At the last *WTC* event they'd collected designer clothes for welfare mothers seeking job interviews. *Why not help them get the interviews first,* Olivia had thought, not that she'd dared ask. Olivia had found that endeavor especially painful. The other *WTC* members had clutched their clothes to their chests with pained expressions, as though they'd even dream of wearing that 1982 Laura Ashley English garden empire waist dress or threadbare old lady St. John suit again, then grudgingly place them into the collection box. "Oh, well," they'd quip, feigning their indifferences. Olivia had rolled her eyes—all that drama, when half the items could have doubled as kitchen towels.

Once, many years earlier, Olivia had suggested the *Collective* focus on more meaningful, interactive projects, but her ideas for tutoring and empowerment workshops had been quickly dismissed. One-on-one involvement with actual needy human beings, she came to understand, wasn't as attractive an idea as, say, *Poker Night for ADHD Awareness* or the *Boots and Bowtie Sobriety Blowout* for the *all-expense paid, 30-day retreat to the luxe California drug rehab of choice!* Drinking martinis in a faux casino and donning sequin-encrusted Stetsons were far more effective, at least according to her *Collective* sisters. The *WTC* was almost sorority worthy. Shit, maybe they should have their Greek alphabet letters plastered across their asses like real sorority girls did. "But, of course, we value one-on-one outreach." Mitzi Rembaucker had told her as a consolation. "That's exactly why we have the *Christmas Exchange*!" Olivia had smiled through her internal groan, vowing never to make another suggestion.

The Christmas Exchange, Olivia's most despised holiday event, was when Prada-clad *WTC* members played Secret Santa to a randomly-chosen child-in-need—though, *randomly-chosen* might be interpreted loosely, as Olivia had seen women sift through the name box for the cute sounding kids, aka, less *cityfied.* Either way, come mid-December, the *Collective* women would gather with their assigned chiding, offering up altruistic smiles as they flung aside raffia ribbons and Bloomies boxes to find . . . the last thing a kid wanted in a Christmas gift.

"I'll get my ass kicked if I wear this!" a boy had shrieked once. Miniature Brooks Brothers khakis crumpled in his one fist and a junior-sized, light blue button-down oxford shirt in the other. "They got returns or what?" Next to Olivia, Gwynnie had snorted, Olivia shooting her a glare.

"Whatever," Gwynnie had muttered. "Seriously, mom, the kid's got a point."

Secretly, Olivia had agreed, taking comfort in the fact that at least their *Christmas Exchanged* child seemed happy. Eight-year-old Mikkie, who, at that very moment, had been whooping, navigating his new remote-controlled mini-monster truck through dismissed Cole-Hahn loafers and bright orange Vilebrequin swimming trunks. *"C'mon, you know I'm right,"* Gwynnie had muttered. *"This is elitist BS."*

Olivia knew where Gwynnie was coming from. She hated every moment of her decade-long inclusion in the *Collective* but sucked it up for Edwin's sake. In fact, he'd been the instigator of her inclusion in the first place. While he would have preferred a more exclusive organization—the *Daughters of the American Revolution*, for instance, that wasn't about to happen considering his wife's background. Not that Olivia flaunted her Jewishness, or even regularly practiced her faith. She wasn't hiding anything. In fact, she made a point of dragging Edwin and Gwynnie to Washington Hebrew at least once a year for the Jewish New Year, Rosh Hashanah. "C'mon! It will be fun to listen to the shofar and inspiring to hear the Rabbi's sermon*,"* she would announce as they all headed to the car. "We'll stop for bagels afterwards at Bagels R Us. I hear they have a new birthday cake, flavored cream cheese!"

The *Collective* might not have been top tier, but it was exclusive enough. Edwin had pulled some strings to get his young, non-connected wife a membership bid, calling in a favor to a client's socialite wife. At the time, Olivia had been touched by her newlywed husband's dedication to philanthropy; only later had she understood that membership held husband perks. Turns out, charitable events were a *great place* to hob-knob with potential clients. This was D.C., after all, where personal and professional agendas were as important as the Pope's Christmas Eve address to the masses.

Now, more than a decade later, Olivia was stuck with the *WTC* and was often tasked with aesthetic-based jobs, choosing invitations, creating table centerpieces and designing banners. Anything that was somewhat artsy was totally Olivia. "You just have such great taste!" Mitzi would gush with each new assignment. "You really do. Would you mind terribly, darling?"

"I'd be happy to help!" Olivia always replied, her plastered-on smile never wavering. *Good thing I used my teeth whitening strips last night!* was often her afterthought.

As if she had an option to not volunteer? With that in mind, at 8:55 a.m., Olivia got out of the car and headed towards Copenhaver. That day, the invitation process seemed to drag even by the *WTC's* usual time-suckage standards. The saleswoman threw out a million questions; "What was the theme? Is there a specific color?" Pertaining to the borders, was she envisioning a swirl or more straight lines? And for the cardstock, did she want basic, cover paper or paperboard? Then, there is the decision on printing. The *WTC* only used engraving, but perhaps it was time for a change? "Thermography? Embossing? Foil stamping or letterpress?" But finally, after what felt like an eternity, the order was officially placed. $3800.00 for custom invites. Outrageous. And that didn't even include postage or the calligrapher for hand addressing.

Exhausted and bored, she was off to her next appointment—her bi-weekly personal training session with Miguel! This kind of obligation fell under the *Physical Maintenance* category. Self-care, some women called it, but to Olivia, it was more *self-preservation* without the embalming fluid. Though, sometimes she thinks drinking the fluid would be so much faster and easier. No parking headaches at least.

After graduating college, and when Olivia first moved to D.C., it hadn't taken her long to understand the city's genetics. Unlike the eccentric Long Island vibe of her youth, this town was more uptight than even the most conservative Capitol Hill congressional caucus. In those early days when she was hopping temp jobs, she'd been surprised by the locals. Not only by the overly serious businessmen for whom she answered phones, but for the supporting characters in their lives. *The Wives and Girlfriends*.

She only met these women on the rare occasions when they stopped by the office, but she found them totally fascinating. They were painstakingly groomed, icy women in boring ensembles that probably cost her monthly rent. Unlike the wealthy, upper-class Jewish mothers of her youth, the M.O. did not embrace a *flaunt-it-if-you-got-it* aesthetic. Her own mother, Gladys, was unique in her elegant, understated style, though her friends were far less subtle. The newest car, the biggest diamond, the most current Chanel or Hermes bag. A sequin here, some fur trim there—not Olivia's taste, but somehow through the materialism, she had grown to appreciate the unapologetic and gaudy showmanship.

Still in her early twenties, Olivia was just finding her footing in the world, but her innate style was obvious. While her wardrobe wasn't *hot-off-the-runway-haute couture*—she mixed classic pieces like her mother's vintage designer hand-me-downs, and items curated from online sales and upscale secondhand establishments. Olivia was undeniably sophisticated with a rock and roll vibe. Upon meeting her, the *Girlfriends and Wives* would often become even icier—if that was possible—offering clipped greetings and bone breaking handshakes. They were ferociously jealous of her intimidating height and charm.

Olivia unknowingly started her final temp job, filling in for an administrative assistant on pregnancy leave at D.C.'s most powerful up-and-coming branding firm, Wyatt Enterprises. Little did she know what would eventually and ultimately transpire from her first day at work.

Now, years later, headed to one of her bi-weekly workout sessions, Olivia had come to understand these women better. Now she was a *Wife* and realized image was everything. To her, the latter was total bullshit. *Who gives a shit about image?* And "image" certainly didn't make her happy . . . anymore.

There were the blow dry appointments. The hair color appointments every six weeks to cover grays and get her perfect blend of crisp ash blonde highlights contrasting against her brown base. Olivia had standing appointments at George's—the salon at the Four Seasons hotel, and often thought of these lost hours as the adult version of a time-out. The *electric chair*, she'd call the salon seat, to which her stylist Ismael would giggle. "You're a riot!" The foils, balayage, root color, glossing, conditioning, toning . . . back to the shampoo bowl for an additional rinse . . . a quick blow dry and finally Ismael's brilliant styling only he could achieve. She always left exhausted and ready for an afternoon cocktail.

Olivia had standing appointments with Miguel. An exclusive, costly training private gym, Georgetown Sweat, a go-to for women of a certain set. The lauded personal trainers were only half the draw. Those millennial, model-quality trainers, come to find out, were known for offering more *extensive services*. But unlike the Sweat cougar contingent, the last thing Olivia wanted was a bodily fluid tryst in the reiki rooms with some gym rat gigolo. Perhaps that's why her own trainer, Miguel, was perfect—*gay, funny and fabulous!*

Sometimes, Olivia thought she *should just have a gay live-in "husband" who could have his own real live-in husband.* No doubt conversation would always be deeply hysterical, she was sure.

Even more, Miguel did little to hide his contempt for the clientele. "Is that the best you can do?" He'd often ask Olivia, then roll his eyes and jack up the incline on her treadmill. "Let's put in some effort here, shall we? If you want a tighter ass . . . run faster! FASTER!!"

Miguel often insulted Sweats' wealthy, demanding clients, seemingly unfazed by the possibility of being fired. "Oh God," he'd grumble, as an infamous billion-aire-wife walked past flirting with her trainer. "Has she seen her face lately? The plastic surgeon must have op-erated in the dark!" Olivia, who had grown accustomed to people hiding their feelings beneath false praise and plastic smiles, found his candor oddly refreshing. Even more, she was tighter and more toned at forty-six than she'd ever been.

Naturally fit, Olivia had maintained a size 4/6 throughout her marriage, but that had grown difficult over time. Pregnancy, a decade of rich gala dinners and endless calorie-laden champagne toasts had creeped up on her. Surprisingly enough, she'd come to enjoy her fitness routine. At first, she'd gone the classic calorie-burning methods, indulging in the latest workout-of-the-week, from hula-hoop hustle to cardio striptease. Ultimately, she'd been put off by the absurdity, embarrassing and strange, cult-like devotion—grown women begging for a spot in Twerk Fitness. Not to mention, watching them shoving and sprinting towards a front row spinning bike at Capitol Spirit Whirler. She wondered if *maybe it was time to finally get a Peloton.*

Those early days of solitary runs weren't without cramping or huffing and puffing for air, but soon enough she gained endurance. Now, her weekly 5k runs weren't just exercise, but a type of meditation too—Olivia loved feeling her muscles beneath the skin, and the echoing sound of her custom Nikes with every thump on the pavement. Only when she was racing towards nowhere, heart pumping and slick with sweat, could Olivia truly empty her mind of all thoughts.

Olivia could not pinpoint when the noise in her head began, exactly—when Edwin increased his business travel? When the bed was more often half-empty than not? When, exactly, had he begun to withdraw, seemingly growing more emotionally absent every day?

Whatever the reason, the worries were hard to ignore, arriving fast and furious. A sudden, unrelenting firing squad in her brain, her own thoughts, and few options for momentary relief. Pop an Ambien, crack a bottle of wine, even volunteer more time at the *WTC* . .

. pack her schedule so tightly there was no room to breathe. Or think, more importantly. Of course, there was one tried and true relief. Perhaps not a cure per se, but for a short time, it felt that way.

Here I come, Miguel, Olivia had thought, starting up the car in the Copenhaver parking lot. That's when she noticed the time—had she miscalculated, rushing through cardstock? She was running 90 minutes early. *A free hour and a half? Jeez. What can I do . . .?* Olivia contemplated her options.

Though, truth be told, by that time her car was already moving towards the parking lot exit and making a right, as though it knew the next destination all on its own. And it wasn't even on auto-drive.

15 minutes later, she parked . . . practically not even realizing how she got there. *What in the world? I don't even remember driving here . . .* Sitting for a minute to collect herself, she looked around and shook her head trying to come back to the reality of the moment. Then, grabbing her remaining cold Starbucks coffee, she made sure she had her purse and phone before stepping out of the car, and slammed the door closely behind her. Olivia's feet had begun moving, like a strange magnetic forcefield, something drawing her through the front glass doors, down one corridor, up an escalator, and down another hallway. She hadn't a plan of where she

intended to go, but suddenly she was there. She looked up and over her head, the clean white sign with crisp black capital lettering she knew all too well. Another home away from her own.

CHANEL

Imaginary Parisian angels started singing as ghost-like images of Coco herself wafted through the door-way. Olivia's body seemed to grow lighter. She stood there for a second, luxuriating in the aura of Coco, the gleaming white marble floors, clear glass countertops and murmured voices. The air smelled of Les Exclusifs de Chanel and retail promise. Her heart fluttered.

Olivia had taken her time, contemplating each dis-play, beautifully glowing under the golden spotlights. Some items familiar, like old friends. Others, unex-pected as a mistress at a Georgetown N Street dinner party. That's one of the things Olivia loved most about fashion—the mystery of the reinvention. In the fashion world, there was always a new beginning right around the corner. New trends, new colors, collections and col-laborations. New faces. New everything.

Olivia wandered from shoes to small accessories, al-lowing the details to catch her eye and absorb into her soul. The textured silver and rich brown suede of the two-tone, cap toed ballet flats, like a whimsical inside joke. And the pumps with their Chanel-esque black and beige color combination—pure ecstasy! A blue leather belt, the buckle a metallic studded starburst, and scarves with their unexpected designs and surprising explosions of color. Olivia ran her hand along the length of one—like a river, the Seine she dreamed, of colorful silk against her skin. Not to mention the earrings, cuffs, pins and necklaces. Retail porn!

And finally, the purses.

Her favorite part of the store, they beckoned her one by one. Every single one. Brand new, yet eternal. They called to her with their twisted locks and chain-link straps, their elegant hardware and finely stitched quilting. Hobos, double flapped clutches and Boy bags (referenced after Coco's pet name she gave to her beloved lover), each a universe into itself. Some were pearl-encrusted daintiness, others lady-like tweed throwbacks; there were bags for jetting to Turks and Caicos, and the refined clutches for tea at the Ritz, 15 Place Vendome. Each one, like a new beginning. New possibilities. New places to go, perhaps, maybe into a new and secret world, waiting in between the petals of the infamous Chanel camellia flower. Olivia's perfect wonderland.

And top of the pyramid? Peering back at her was gorgeous perfection, The Queen herself. La Reine. *The 2.55.*

No need to inquire; Olivia knew the bag on sight. Double-flapped, black caviar leather and silver hardware. She'd leaned in, noting the details, inhaling the soft leather scent—the tiny, precise stitches on the diamond quilting, the chain strap threaded with delicate leather. And prominently facing-out, front and center? That iconic and original Mademoiselle clasp. (Later, and under Karl's direction in the early 1980's, the bag was updated adding a clasp with the infamous CC's interlocking in perfect harmony.)

This wasn't a purse; this was a purse incarnate. A legend. Like Coco herself. According to mythology, Gabrielle "Coco" Chanel had grown tired of carrying handbags on her arms. So, taking inspiration from the long-strapped bags of soldiers, she created the infamous 2.55, freeing up her arms and hands. The bag was named for the month and year in which it was originally created, February 1955. The interior, burgundy in color, representing the color of the uniforms at the convent where Coco was raised; the quilt pattern on the leather is believed to have been inspired by cushions in her Paris apartment. With the 2.55, women could clink champagne glasses, make sweeping gestures or even give an illicit hand job under the table if so desired. With one long chain hanging over their shoulder or crossing their bosom, voila, they were suddenly hands-free.

Perhaps not the most fiscally healthy outlet, these shopping excursions, but it could have been worse. Half the women in Georgetown were puking up their food, popping Oxy or fucking some version of a Sweat trainer. So, she liked nice things. There were worse outlets, that's what she told herself. And no prescription or exclusive wine label in the world, Olivia had come to believe, could offer quite the same high. Watching a saleswoman ring up new Manolo BB pumps or tenderly tissue wrap a Michael Kors collection cashmere sheath, Olivia would feel a sudden lightness in her limbs, a tingling from flamingo pink painted toenails to ash blonde colored hair follicles.

But not the 2.55. It was even bigger than that. She felt as if her head were going to blow off her shoulders.

"Lovely, isn't it?" The voice had startled Olivia from her 2.55 induced fever dream. A young sales lady had beamed, her face pulled tightly around a well-practiced smile.

"This purse is iconic. Coco Chanel herself."

"I know all that," said Olivia. That's when she suddenly realized. It had been a dark revelation, but one of which, she was sure.

Edwin would never buy her this bag, no matter how many hints she dropped. She couldn't have made the hints any more obvious. Photos texted to his phone, emailed to his personal account, sent to his personal assistant when she hinted at what Olivia wanted for her birthday from Edwin. Olivia even took her husband into the CHANEL boutique and introduced him to her friend, Marty, the store Director. Olivia was destined to go from appointment to appointment, task to task, 2.55-less, for the rest of eternity. Finally, she decided to take the plunge.

"I'll take it in black," Olivia said. "But quickly, please. I'm on my way to a personal training appointment. And you know what? I want a second, in camel, too." *WTF. And, fuck Edwin, too. Self-serving asshole!*

As quickly and unwittingly as she had arrived, she found herself back in the parking lot, staring, blankly, at the 2.55s in the car's front passenger seat. They were like little newborn babies swaddled and buckled in ever so carefully. What had she done? It happened so fast! Just like that, a few minutes and $19,000 and change later, Olivia was the new owner of a bag, two in fact, that she'd coveted for as long as she could remember. She should have felt the usual burst of adrenaline, the guilt-tinged high. That giddy, all-encompassing retail rush only magnified. She should have been popping champagne, her favorite Moncuit, and feeling lighter than air.

Instead, she felt . . . strangely empty.

That's when the phone rang. Olivia had lunged for her cell, welcoming the distraction—*good God what now? An issue with the WTC? The caterer wasn't working out, the tablecloths hadn't arrived, the flowers were wilted.* Along with her busy schedule, these sorts of emergencies were frequent. She found a way to handle them every time, without missing a beat—or an appointment.

The name on the screen stopped her cold.

Gaining control, she managed to hang on to the phone. "Edwin," she said frantically. *Did he get a text notifying him of the CHANEL purchase or something?* She figured he was open about her buying the bag but did demonstrate finance controlling tendencies from time to time. And shit, she had bought two. "Are you okay?"

"Sure," he'd said. "Why?"

Olivia sighed, choosing not to dignify that with an answer. Three days since he left for his business trip, and not a word. Unless you count the text, *I landed.*

"Olivia, I need your help."

No hello or I miss you. No inquiries into how she was feeling, sharing of his location or even a mention of

Gwynnie. Just Edwin, launching right in. Going right for the kill, as he was famous for doing.

"A dinner party," he said. "Last minute, I know, but I need your magic. Make it for seven o'clock. Yes, champagne at seven . . . I land at five, so that'll give me plenty of time to get home. And I need you to go all out on this one, okay? I'm talking seriously . . . epic."

Olivia sighed, officially annoyed. He was to land on Sunday. That was two days from now. What was he thinking?

Edwin wasn't thinking at all; he was too busy talking.

"Drake Robinson. He's only in town for one night. I just got the call. And then I told him are you kidding me, man? We gotta get together! I'll have Olivia pull together one of her astronomical dinner parties!"

Edwin went on and on, showcasing the sense of urgency, though Olivia didn't know what the situation was, exactly. From what she could gather, Drake-something was coming to town, and he was important, though Olivia had no earthly idea who he might be, or why he mattered or for what reason she should give a shit. And Drake-something deserved a dinner party. Not just any dinner party, but a *seriously-epic-fucking-dinner-party* that Edwin expected Olivia to plan, execute and pull off . . . by *Sunday*.

"This guy is the real deal," Edwin had said. A total thought leader. On the cutting edge of targeted rebranding . . ."

Olivia didn't have the faintest idea what Edwin was talking about. She sat in the car listening to her husband rant and babble on about *strategic integration* and *killer funding*, all the time imagining the 2.55s, snugly waiting in their black ribboned boxes. Her gorgeous Chanel newborns. That's when the realization hit her.

Olivia had no earthly idea who her husband was anymore.

Sure, she knew the basics about Edwin. She knew he liked his Hästens mattress firm and that he preferred *Fortune* to *Businessweek*. She knew the size of his dick (definitely smaller than average, though she hadn't seen it for herself in 22 days) and how he took his coffee (two Sweet and Lows, a splash of cream). She knew his slow, charming grin—she saw it often on her daughter's face—and that Rothko was his favorite artist, only because they owned one, a purchase that had been made as an investment. She was aware of his official job title, of course, as was every other D.C. insider: *Edwin Wyatt, CEO of Wyatt Enterprises.* Just like them, she knew this billion-dollar operation branded major entities, including retail chains, high-level personalities and titans of industry. She was aware of his reputation for creating innovative and intoxicating campaigns, raising profiles and bringing in capital. How he did that, exactly, was bathed in mystery. She'd long ago stopped asking, let alone caring. *He's huge, Olivia. Seriously crushing the silicon market . . .*

Ten years older than she, when they first met, Edwin struck Olivia as light years ahead of the men she usually dated—mostly eager, twenty-something Ivy alums toting shiny new MBA's and recently acquired positions at massive corporate entities. Before that temp job at Wyatt Enterprises, these were the men she dated, and the ones she tried to extract interesting information from, which often felt like squeezing water from a rock. When queried about their professional lives, most of the time, their eyes would go glassy. They'd sigh, talking vaguely of long hours at the office and bulked up stock and real estate portfolios, seeming even more bored by their work than Olivia was of them. What they really cared about, Olivia had come to realize, was their golf game, or wine-collecting hobby. Beer hops percentages, sports scores and playing show-and-tell with their latest toy. "I just got a new seven series," they'd say, faces lighting up. "Did I tell you? And did I mention my new beach house?" The reality was usually a lease on a used early 2000's model and a ratty time share in the Outer Banks, but that didn't matter. Olivia longed for something more.

Then, Edwin had walked into her life, like a breath of the freshest Swiss snow-capped mountain air. In their courtship, and during those first several years of marriage, Edwin shared all his business exploits and endeavors, even asking for her opinion. "What do you think of this logo?" he'd say. "The color blend ombre technique?" She'd answer honestly, and he'd often take the advice. "Sharp eye," he'd say. "Why am I paying some bullshit art director 100k when I got you?" They'd talk about what she could do with that talent. Maybe interior design, or something in fashion. Edwin understood that and nurtured the possibilities. "You've got talent, baby. You just gotta figure out what you want to do with it."

But that was a long time ago. Before he proposed. Before the enormous wedding to plan, before they bought the Georgetown townhouse, which required outrageous and extensive renovations. Before the *WTC* weekly meetings, and the centerpieces in need of designing. Before the traveling started, and before the long hours, the moody spells and distant eyes. That was before he landed NASCAR, his biggest client ever.

Olivia refocused her attention back to Edwin. "See if you can get some VIP's. One of the Senators, maybe.

The Brazilian Ambassador for sure, he's always up for a good time."

She wondered where Edwin was calling from. A hotel . . . somewhere nice, of course. The Mandarin maybe. Did they have that hotel in Daytona? Or maybe he was touring the racetrack—she could swear there was the distant hum of an engine—or perhaps he was at NASCAR headquarters. Maybe he'd spent the morning sitting in conference rooms full of serious-looking corporate types going over numbers and analyzing charts. Olivia had long ago stopped asking what his job really entailed. Perhaps "prepping a campaign" meant bro-bonding with testosterone-fueled execs, a.k.a. eating steak, downing shots and stuffing wrinkled dollar bills into skanky South Beach stripper G-strings. Shit, for all she knew, he and those NASCAR dudes could be pushing toy cars across a boardroom table, giggling like little boys, *vroom vroom*ing and calling it market research.

What she knew right then was that her appointment with Miguel started in ten minutes, she was going to be late, and this call would fuck up her entire day's schedule for sure. Oh, and she somehow wound up with two 2.55s sitting in the car seat next to her.

"I get it, Edwin," she said. "A dinner party on Sunday. I'll make it happen. But I've got to go or I'm . . ."

"Sunday? Did you hear a word I just said?" Suddenly, Edwin sounded annoyed. "Tonight Olivia. This is happening tonight." Then, voice low and oozing gruff charm. "I know you can pull it off, baby."

There was no time to be annoyed, let alone angry. Edwin had pulled this shit on her before. It wasn't unusual to get this request or announcement at least once weekly, "We've got eight people coming at 7:30 p.m. What can you whip up? Sorry, today was nuts! I didn't even get a minute to shoot you a text." She had Edwin's number by now, though she truly was considering deleting it and moving on. She had never even thought about divorce until recently. Years of living with a narcissist jerk was finally catching up to her.

After a quick call to cancel Miguel, (never mind the late cancel fee, $175!) Olivia goes into hyper AAA-focused mode. *Food, liquor, flowers,* she thinks, while simultaneously driving and calling out contacts for Siri to dial. *I'll call in last-minute orders, send Claudia to the grocery store, make sure the house is clean*—she runs through the to-do list in her head while leaving voicemails with her most charming, ingratiating pitch. "Please come for champagne at 7:00 . . . last minute dinner party, VIPs . . . impressive guest list . . . it'll be fabulous!"

The problem was, D.C. didn't do last-minute, thrown-together anything. At least not in the Wyatt circle. Details were much more important to handle than risking a last-minute fumble. The one person she reached, the wife of Edwin's client, was confused. "We'd love to, but . . . did you say *tonight*?" She'd asked incredulously. "Oh, I'm sorry Olivia, we have this thing at the Society of the Cincinnati . . ."

Amongst Edwin and Olivia's set, social gatherings weren't an after school extracurricular activity, but a lifestyle necessity. They were a means of career advancement, an opportunity to network, a chance to be seen by all the right people or, even better, be the right people others were hoping to see. Every night in D.C. was a black tie, diplomatic dinner party, charity ball or fundraiser, and in between were the informal yet equally mandatory dinner parties, meet-and-greets, cocktail parties and get-togethers. No pinball and peanut-littered floor for this crowd; even impromptu happy hours must take on larger social connotations, a sense of legacy. The location also had to offer significant connotations, exclusivity or historic sex appeal. Forget downing frozen daiquiris at a suburban Outback. Meeting at the Hay Adams bar with the award-winning mixologist, or Martin's Tavern, where JFK proposed to Jackie, were more acceptable public locales in this strict culture.

Those calls on the ride home had proven unsuccessful, but failure was not an option. Finally, at home, she'd quickly raced upstairs, shoving her new Chanel babies, still in their boxes and wrapped in crisp white ribbon, to the back of her closet. *Time to get serious,* she thought.

Who owes me a favor? Who wants to get in Edwin's good graces? Who can I count on as a truly loyal friend? Time for a serious D.C. Quid Pro Quo, assholes. Just you wait, Edwin, you fucking and inconsiderate bastard, she thought, flipping through her contact list. *I'll give you your pathetic, boring and seriously epic dinner party.*

Chapter Three

Where's Edwin?

7:45 p.m.

Somehow, she pulled it off. Olivia scans the living room, focusing momentarily on the mingling guests, thinking *I'm good. Really good.* She is also reminded, once again, that her husband's name holds serious weight. Enough that plans can be canceled, and schedules rearranged. Inconvenience could be overlooked, it seems, when incurred by a Very Important Prick.

Olivia covertly circulates the room, doing the required check-in . . . the recessed lights had been atmospherically dimmed, the Dyptique candles lit, and Billie Holiday cued up on the Bose sound system. All champagne glasses were filled. Heavy hors-d'oeuvres circulated, as hands dipped into crystal bowls full of gourmet salted Virginia peanuts, a mandatory staple with this crowd, a weird D.C. quirk Olivia would never understand. Her eyes scan from guest to guest, taking inventory. Still early enough, yet everyone had arrived.

Mostly.

She checks the antique German Cuckoo clock. *8:15 p.m.*

Time for guest list inventory, she decides.

By the Steinway, the senior Lobbyist and Journalist are well into heated conversation, their cocktails refreshed. The Lobbyist is a yoga-enthusiast, cleanse-junkie divorcee—the kind who won't just march for Women's Rights, but who also swears by her vaginal steaming treatments. "Like a mini gynecologist, really. The V-Steam cocktail parties are the best!" She disdains patriarchy, hence her single status. The Journalist is her polar-opposite, turning think-pieces for a notoriously conservative online journal, and living in the conservative version of a bachelor pad with a framed Regan portrait adorning the wall. Yet the chemistry is clear—come midnight, they'll be hate-fucking. Olivia would put money on it. Not only had she landed great guests, but she also made unintentional love connections.

Lobbyist, check. Journalist, check.

Across the room, The Diplomat holds court on the cognac colored leather couch, entertaining with tales of memorable diplomatic endeavors. The time he went on a date with Princess Diana, perhaps, or got stuck in Gambia during a coup. The Society Matron is there, listening intently, as is the up-and-coming, buzzworthy female painter—her token Artsy Type, a necessity at every D.C. party. She'd learned long ago, no matter how boring the guests, an Artsy Type will keep things moving. *You do what? Oh, that's so interesting! You do that . . . as a career? I figured because you had a tattoo you were unemployed!* And the Diplomat, for one, is absolutely intrigued—perhaps more for her low-cut dress than her canvas know-how. Either way, the group is getting along splendidly—the Diplomat charms, the Painter fawns and the Society Matron flirts outrageously.

Check, check, check.

The Diplomat's plus-one . . . or minus, as Olivia sees her . . . has disappeared. A tall, red-haired eastern European model type who barely speaks English, Olivia has the sneaking suspicion this so-called-date gets paid by the hour. Olivia has no idea where she might have gone—probably snorting lines or smoking in the bathroom—but chooses not to worry about it. When it comes to The Potential Escort, out-of-sight and out-of-mind seems the way to go.

OK, Moving on.

The Lawyer and Gas Heir are at the wet bar, sipping on their drinks, while their Wives stand nearby, politely conversing while simultaneously side-eyeing all the other attendees. The Lawyer is a genius having recently settled a copyright infringement case for millions, and the Heir, one of those charming bougie types, is most likely gearing up for another adventure to who knows where. Perhaps heliskiing the Icelandic tundra or tracking mountain gorillas in Rwanda. Friends of Edwin, both men are extraordinary. And their Wives? Unfortunate excess baggage. And not even designer at that . . . we're talking about used and abused old school Samsonite.

Given other circumstances, Olivia avoids socializing with their variety of Wives as much as possible, but she needed the last-minute bodies. They'd been more than happy to oblige the rare invitation, jumping on the coveted opportunity to see the Wyatt's six-bedroom, Georgetown 18th century federal townhouse. Now, she watches as they greedily take in their surroundings, doing a mental *Price Is Right: Georgetown Edition* in their heads. Along with noting the monetary expenditure, they are sure to make judgments, carefully taking in the exotic imported furniture, Moroccan silk accents and the sleek black leather Eaves chair and ottoman. Every piece has been carefully chosen by Olivia, picked for its sophistication and elegance, each telling a story. Yet, Olivia knows what they are thinking; to the Wives, the decor is akin to an opium den. The Wives much prefer the uber-expensive, boring-as-hell, as is her name, suburban Interior Designer, Mary Jones, who over-hauled their cookie-cutter Great Falls, Virginia McMansions.

Olivia must admit, for a last-minute, thrown to-gether shindig, the party is proving to be a surprise hit. All guests are accounted for and enjoying themselves immensely . . . with two very notable exceptions. The infamous guest of honor, Drake Robinson, and The Most Powerful, himself—her husband.

In the hour since the party officially began, Olivia has gone from peeved to concerned, to outright worried. The time has come to accept that Edwin is well-past ac-ceptably late. Not knowing where he is or how to get hold of him, Olivia's eyes settle on an empty cham-pagne bottle atop their mid-century French console. She grabs it and nonchalantly heads for the hallway, the drained Moncuit bottle clutched in one hand and cell phone in the other.   She'll call him again. He's bound to pick up this time. Perhaps the cell was out of juice . . . he just needed to charge it.   There, once again, she lists off the possibilities in her head. Dead phone, traffic jam, delayed flight. She starts to dial Edwin's cell when she suddenly hears something.

"DAH-ling!" rings out a voice. "Where have you been, lovey?"

One foot through the alcove, Olivia freezes, forces a smile and turns, just in time to see Daphne Davenport gliding towards her. Daphne, face glowing, bangles tinkling, and cashmere wrap fluttering, sweeps down the hallway as though walking a Milan runway, instead of a fully restored Georgetown hardwood floor entryway.

Legendary socialite, society maven . . . yet, unlike the other guests, Daphne could never be reduced to a title. She was the one call Olivia had looked forward to, and the one that had not required faux enthusiasm. "A last-minute dinner party," she'd simply said. "Edwin threw this shit on me. Again."

"Say no more," Daphne had responded. "I'll cancel everything. What time do you need me?"

A glamourous fixture on the Georgetown circuit, Daphne's age bracket is as mysterious as her frequent travel—though rumor has it she's seventy-something—Olivia often suspects those Brazilian excursions might truthfully be of the plastic surgeon holiday variety. Either way, Olivia has always adored the quirky, formidable force-of-nature, and finds herself unexpectedly comforted by Daphne's familiar, warm smile.

"Ollliiivia," trilled Daphne. A double air kiss through Dior red lips, then a narrowing of the eyes. "Where in the goddamn hell have you been?" She gazes at Olivia and knows something isn't right. After all these years, Daphne still has a way of seeing right through her. Olivia maintains the plastered-on smile through a long sigh. "It has been a lot of stress, putting this damn thing together last minute."

"Darling, of course it has! You must be worn out! But you don't look exhausted, not at all. In fact, lovey, you look scrumptious! Turn around for me now, won't you? Oh, to have my forty-six-year-old tits back! Do you mind if I touch them? Just sublime! But tell me, how have you been?"

Despite her stress, Olivia cannot help but smile back—this time, for real.

"It's so good to see you, too. And . . . I'm just fine. I'm wonderful in fact!"

"Wonderful," Daphne repeats, then goes quiet. For a moment, she just stares at Olivia. "Bullshit." Says Daphne. "How long have I known you, darling?"

Olivia feels naked beneath Daphne's sharp gaze, remembering how much the elder woman has done for her. Olivia had felt like an outsider until Daphne took a liking to her. The society matron had swept the young wife into her *J'adore Dior* "parfum-ed" web, making the rounds with her *much* younger protegee. Why she had chosen to embrace Olivia out of all the young Wives—a revolving door of them in this city—remained a mystery. Perhaps she'd seen a bit of herself in the young woman—a fish out of water, but unmistaka-bly independent. "You have a fire," Daphne once sur-mised, "smoldering beneath that finely polished surface."

"Where exactly is Edwin?" says Daphne, getting straight to the point.

"Oh, just running late," says Olivia, straining to keep her voice light and normal sounding. "I'm sure he'll be storming through the door any minute."

"I see," says Daphne. "Due to the recent brow lift and Tuesday's Botox injections, I am incapable of rais-ing my eyebrows. But please note, Olivia, you know I am not buying that."

Olivia attempts a lighthearted laugh. "Oh, Daphne, please. Everything is fine!"

"So, judging by his tardiness one might assume Ed-win is busier than ever. Am I correct?"

"Well, he just landed a big account with . . ."

"Yes, exactly. And while it isn't easy, having an absentee husband . . . there are some perks that should be acknowledged. The luxury of free time, for one. Do you not agree?"

Olivia knows this is a rhetorical question.

"Expendable hours are a gift, my lovely, and your various skills are far too valuable to keep to yourself.

You should start a design business, as I've always said. And now is the time! Isn't that a marvelous idea?"

Olivia mentioned the idea more than a decade ago, saying perhaps she wanted to start an interior design business. But then came Gwendolyn, and the *WTC Collective.* And galas, hair and nail appointments, personal training sessions . . . non-stop personal and superficial physical upkeep. That was what became of her. It all became her job.

Daphne remembered, and even more, thought to bring it up at this very moment.

"Oh, I'm so busy," said Olivia.

"Oh, come on! It would be a breeze! Besides, you have experience. You did it professionally!"

"Well, that was fashion, not design. And professionally is really pushing it. I was an assistant for a designer, just briefly, and worked a little retail. But I . . ."

"Oh, tomato-tomahto and who gives a fuck?" Daphne leans in, voice lowered. "What I'm saying, darling, is that you need an outlet. Don't take this the wrong way, you look lovely, but you also have a very negative and depressing aura. There's something in your eyes, something I don't like. A dullness. You know I speak my mind, especially when it comes to you. And I see you so infrequently now, which I don't like either. By the way, you never answered my question. Where *is* Edwin?"

"I told you, he's just . . ."

"Yes, yes. Late, I remember. For the last-minute dinner party that he, himself requested. Basically, demanded. (Insert challenged eyebrow raise.) Oh, fine, fine. Go on now. I see you are just tolerating my nosiness, and I am out of line, I know that" she says, waving Olivia off. "None of this is my business, I am well-aware. All I'm saying is that, if the need arose, it could be a reality. You've got what it takes, Olivia. It's inborn with you."

A pointed look, three quick air kisses and just like that, Daphne turns abruptly, already calling towards the living room "Oh Matteo!" she sings as she struts down the hallway. "You must tell me more of your stories!" A wink over her shoulder to Olivia, and she disappears through the doorway. Olivia can picture her sweeping towards the oversized white canvas couch, and directly to the grinning Armani-clad Italian diplomat. He'll already be standing to offer her a seat, ready to regale her with his charming stories. Matteo lived for entertaining attractive women regardless of relationship status or age bracket. Olivia thinks of that table they shared at a *WTC* fundraiser several years ago—was it for *First World Suburban Lyme Disease?   Emergency Jack Russell*

Terrier Training?—and how he flirted with her shame-lessly all evening. She liked the attention but would have enjoyed it more had Edwin noticed. Later, when Olivia mentioned it in their private car ride home, he'd simply shrugged. "He's Italian."

Just like that, her agitation is back, with waves of panic, growing closer to the shore. Olivia turns with quick determination, ducking into a darkened alcove, she dials Edwin.

Voicemail. *Again.*

"Seriously Edwin?!" Olivia says into the phone, her voice high with anxiety. "I'm really pissed now. I called the airport . . . they said the plane landed, though they wouldn't tell me if you were on the flight, so . . . where are you? I'm getting seriously . . . well . . . just call me back!"

She hangs up abruptly and leans against the wall, checking the time.

8:45 p.m.

The plane landed more than two hours ago. Even with traffic, a baggage mix-up, or even a last-minute cli-ent emergency, Edwin had more than enough time to make it from Reagan National Airport to Georgetown, change and greet the guests. She'd even picked his out-fit—black dress pants, Gucci loafers and his Japanese cotton tailor-made, teal button-down shirt. Only he wasn't here, and the freshly dry-cleaned garments were upstairs, hanging untouched in his custom designed walk-in closet.

She'd called the Wyatt offices, praying a straggling employee might be pulling a late-night deadline. Nada. She'd considered contacting the VIP Guest of Honor, also MIA, though she had no information on how to reach him. Edwin said he'd be staying in D.C. that night, so chances are he'd possibly already arrived and checked in . . . but where? Based on the quick google search of his name it could be anything from a five-star hotel to a crappy youth hostel. Robinson was one of those renegade Silicon Valley guys who reveled in shaking up the system, being unpredictable.

Of all of Edwin's clients, Olivia finds these tech wunderkinds the most tiresome, with their billion-dollar portfolios, Vans sneakers and bizarre quirks. Still, she had taken the leap, trying a few places he might be—the Four Seasons, the Georgetown Ritz, Café Milano. Maybe he was with some woman du moment or possibly even an airbnb in the Virginia or Maryland suburbs. No luck and no telling where he might be.

She'd already gone so far as to call Millennial #1 and Millennial #2—aka, Edwin's first and second assistant. Millennial #1 was no longer with the company, she had informed Olivia chirpily, saying she'd quit for another job. "Event publicity!" She'd explained. "Concerts, fundraisers, big-time promos. Isn't that sick?" Olivia agreed that yes, it was indeed sick, then quickly extricated herself from the conversation.

Millennial #2 went straight to voicemail. "I'm Honeymooning on Maui!" Squealed the voicemail message. "See you bitches when we get back! Mahalo!"

Ugh, Olivia had thought.

And forget any family to call. There weren't many to speak of. Edwin's father was long gone and there were few others to choose from. She figured she would call his half-senile mother, catching her at the nursing home in Boca. Within moments, she'd realized the call was a big mistake. "Olivia who?" The woman asked, then spent three precious minutes complaining about the terrible canned peaches they served for lunch and her untrustworthy nurse, whom she believed to be stealing. "Half my butterscotch candies were gone," she lamented, "and I swear she was wearing my perfume! My favorite too, Giorgio!" Thankfully, the conversation ended soon after; the old lady suddenly convincing herself Olivia was a telemarketer and abruptly hanging up the phone.

A final last-ditch effort, she'd gritted her teeth and dialed Chad Hargrove. Edwin's business partner. Chad's participation in Wyatt Enterprises is more party-worthy than active—meaning they were college buddies. She hadn't been surprised when her call went straight to voicemail. "Heeeeeeey," came Chad's gravelly voice, "Sorry I missed you! But no biggie. Just leave your digits and I'll getcha back soon as . . ."

Olivia hung up, imagining where Edwin might be at that moment. Here she was, desperately trying to find her workaholic husband, while his Head of Operations was most likely spraying champagne from an enormous Moet bottle to thumping music, pulsing strobe lights and oiled up gyrating flesh. Or maybe he was snowboarding in Aspen or wooing girls in Thailand. Either way, it was an act of desperation on her part.

Beeeeep.

A text! Olivia lifts the phone so fast she drops another empty champagne bottle on the Persian carpet.

I'm starrrviiiiingggggggg. Can Claudia bring me a tray please?

You've got legs, writes Olivia, grateful for the interruption.

Ur and Daddy's friends—borrring. I'm so hungry. Omfgggg!

Don't curse, writes Olivia.

Txt speak is viable communication in the digital age, get with it, lady. Puhleeese? So hunnnnngrrry gonna tell the school counselor you turned me anorexic . . .

NOT FUNNY. Okay, okay. I'll send Claudia up in a bit.

Is Daddy back yet?

Not yet. Soon.

K . . . love you mommy! Gwynnie replies, followed by a string of emojis—hearts, happy faces, a dancing owl. Completely nonsensical, but Olivia finds herself smiling. Maybe for the first time all night.

By 9:05, Olivia is ushering guests into the dining room.

"Edwin won't mind. He'd want us to start without him!"

The guests don't mind either, taking their seats, alive with conversation. Olivia can't bring herself to sit in one place, so she keeps herself busy, pacing back and forth to the kitchen, telling Claudia it's fine. "I've got it!" She says, picking up the Italian herbarium hand-painted porcelain serving platter, then returning for the pepper grinder and extra napkins. "Seriously, Claudia, this is too much stress on you, this last-minute stuff . . . let me handle it!"

By 9:15, the buffet is ready. Guests help them-selves, chatting as they spoon out beef tenderloin and risotto onto their simple white plates. Olivia offers the occasional nod or agreement while busily overseeing the refilling of champagne. The mantra continues, only growing darker.

She keeps her smile no matter what. As Matteo tells an off-color story, she smiles. When everyone laughs at the punchline, she joins right in. "Oh, Matteo! You are too much!"

Come 9:35, with everyone eating, she knows her flitting around is starting to look weird. So, Olivia joins them, sitting before her untouched plate, nodding at statements she has not heard, drinking champagne like water. She listens to the hum of conversation, the clinking of silver, and the rising laughter . . . and she knows. It is time to face facts.

Head spinning, Olivia rushes for the first quiet place she can think of: *Edwin's home office.* She races inside, closes the door, and only then, wrapped in that cocoon of mahogany and dark brown leather, does she finally give in to the fear. *This is real*, she thinks. Olivia can't breathe; she feels dizzy.

She falls backwards into the *Armani Casa* leather chair and ottoman, eyes circling the room as she tries to steady herself for the task ahead. She rarely comes in here—no one does, except Claudia for the occasional dusting. The vintage advertisements lining the wall and his cabinet of industry awards. The golf clubs, the Rothko, the retro pinball machine and signed Babe Ruth baseball glove in an air-controlled, lighted acrylic display case. She's never paid much attention to these acquisitions and is surprised by the sheer number of them. The electric guitar signed by Slash, the model race cars, the baseball card collection and Calder mobile. The first edition books—*The Fountainhead, The Sun Also Rises, Ulysses*—not that he'd ever read them. *Some things are for fun*, he once explained, *and some are investments. That's how it is with collecting, Olivia.*

She lifts the phone, takes a deep breath. Dials 9 . . .

"Helllllloooooo! Where have you been?"

Olivia squeals, whipping around to see . . . Gwynnie, standing in the open door, still wearing the skirt from her school uniform. On top, a baggy gray sweatshirt, so big she might drown in it. Only she's cut out the neckline, so it hangs off her bare shoulders, making her look effortlessly disheveled, renegade cool. Her hair is in a messy ponytail, her face makeup-free, her expression that unnerving mix of disdain and amusement only a fifteen-year-old can effectively pull off. Even in that moment, full of frantic apprehension, Olivia is taken by how beautiful she is. This little girl, who is not so little anymore. This almost young woman who is staring at her, eyebrows lifted.

"OMG, Mom. I've been looking everywhere for you," she says, hands on blue pleated hips. "Why are you in here?"

"Oh, just taking a little break, honey!" Olivia answers softly.

There's a pause as Gwynnie contemplates her mother, the annoyance melting into something else—*concern.*

"Mommy? Are you okay?"

"Of course," says Olivia, though it comes out more croak than chirp.

Another pause. Gwynnie isn't buying it.

"Who are you calling?" she says, voice muted, glancing at the phone in Olivia's hand. Then, with a soft voice. "Where's Daddy?"

Olivia opens her mouth, ready with a hundred excuses, only nothing comes out. *Say something,* she thinks, throat constricted. *Tell her he's on his way. Tell her he should arrive any minute.*

And then, out of nowhere, the doorbell rings. Olivia and Gwynnie look at each other. Olivia, full of fear. Gwynnie, excited to finally see her father back home.

"There he is!" Olivia squeals, jumping to her feet, effervescent like imaginary Moncuit champagne bubbles floating up inside of her. *I'm going to fucking kill you, Edwin,* Olivia thinks, opening the front door.

But it isn't Edwin at the door. It's two blue uni-
formed men, badges in hand.

Chapter Four

Home Sweet Home

Two Months Later

"Ollllivvvviaaaa!" The voice rings out. "Olivia, honnnneeey? Are you up?"

Olivia is having that nightmare again. The one in which everything she knows, everything familiar, has suddenly disappeared. The big things, like her home and her friends. Her car. But also, the smaller things. Her Persian rugs and Cartier diamond trinity ring, the Baccarat crystal and Cristofle silver flatware. There are no credit cards in her Prada wallet, nor a Prada wallet to carry them; no shoes lining her walk-in closet, no more purses, Italian cashmeres, Hermes accessories. All the things she's ever owned, even the stuff she never cared about, like Auto-Chill machines purchased in Xanax-induced states. Oh, and there's no Xanax either.

Then the voice comes. Insistent and steady, growing louder and closer . . . more intense . . .

"Olllivvvvvvviaaaa!"

Olivia blinks a few times, her surroundings coming into focus. That's when she realizes: She is right back where she started.

Only half-awake, Olivia looks around, once again startled by how little has truly changed. The room is exactly as it was when she was sixteen. There is her old oak bookcase, stocked with school textbooks, beloved novels and back issues of fashion magazines—*W, Harper's, French Vogue.* Each read cover to cover, dog-eared marking her favorite pages. And there is her teenage desk, with the Tiffany lamp her father Milton bought for her thirteenth birthday.

Milton. She sighs, once again wishing her father was around. Decades since he died of a heart attack, and she's never missed him more.

The walls are plain white, except for the two posters just like she remembered. One was black and white of the Eiffel Tower, finished with a simple black frame, and the other, of Audrey Hepburn, aloof and iconic in classic Givenchy.

That's you, Mrs. Wyatt. The Holly Golightly of Georgetown.

Not anymore, thinks Olivia.

"Ollllivvvvvvviaaaa? It's almost noon!"

That's when it hits her—hits her like a sack of hot shit right out of the bright blue sky above.

This isn't a dream. This is right now. This is Olivia, grown-up. Forty-six-year-old Olivia Wyatt—strike that, Kopelman—in her childhood bedroom. Her bedroom that is precisely the same. It's like taking up residence in a painstakingly maintained monument to the person you once were . . . a person who no longer exists.

"Ollllivvvvvvvvia, it's time to get up!"

And that voice? Gladys herself, standing at the door. Giving her *that* look. The one she remembers so clearly from her teenage years, only right now, completely unchanged.

God, it's not even—Olivia checks her old alarm clock on the nightstand—*8:15 a.m.*, thinks Olivia. But there's Gladys, fresh as a daisy, already primped, polished and primed to take on the world. The vintage tweed Chanel jacket impeccably maintained, tailored exactly to her still-lithe form; her flared beige trousers with creases as sharp as a German Wusthof knife. Dainty leather Belgian loafers, J. Lo/Kim Kardashian-esque-nude lipstick, slightly teased hair and her signature pearls. She's got several sets, each doled out depending on her daily agenda. The double strand is *Hadassah Meeting*, the Japanese cultured is *Bridge Club* and the black Tahitians, *Out on the Town*. Today is freshwater with a pink hue, *Lunch with the Girls*.

"Olivia? Can't you hear me? I've been sympathetic, darling. I mean, I'm practically bleeding sympathy, aren't I? I mean hellllloooo? I've been nurturing and comforting. Haven't said a word about you lying around all the time."

"I wouldn't go that far," mumbles Olivia.

". . . moping hour upon hour. I've let you lick your wounds. Answer me, Olivia."

"Yes, Mom. You've been really . . ."

"I'm not finished. The time has come. Enough. It's time to pick yourself up and look toward the future!"

"Oh God." Olivia silently groans, fighting the urge to pull the white down comforter over her head. *Look toward the future . . . really? The future is as clear as the smog in New Delhi rush hour.*

"So . . ." says her mother, doing that obnoxious mind-reader thing Olivia hates. "What are your plans today? Accomplish something, please? This is getting ridiculous! Olivia, I know you are listening. It's time we talk about things, Olivia. You can't go on like this." Gladys looks at her, waiting for a response.

Seriously Mom? She thinks. "Do we have to do it now?" Questions Olivia.

Olivia knew this was coming. Gladys could only hold her tongue for so long. And Olivia had to hand it to her mother, she'd shown great restraint. When she first heard the news—from the NY Post, of all places (albeit Page 6 at least)— she'd called Olivia right away. "Oh God, Olivia." She'd said nothing when Olivia begged her not to come to the funeral. "It'll be a madhouse, Mom, trust me. As soon as things settle, we'll come see you." Then, when Olivia called from the train station? Gladys hadn't asked questions. "I'll be there in ten," she'd said, only to pull into the parking lot to find Olivia and Gwynnie standing there, surrounded by suitcases. Her daughter and granddaughter, standing close to each other, nowhere to go . . . *yet had she offered up even the slightest critique?*

That's what her mother was thinking, Olivia was sure of it. That she'd been silent, patient as any prophet from the totality of Jewish teaching, culture and practice. Only now, it was enough.

"I repeat, Olivia," she says. "What are your plans?"

Plans? What could she possibly say other than the truth: *the same plans I've had since I got here, Mom!*

Nap, watch TV, shuffle around the house, maybe eat half a yogurt, and if she's feeling especially self-loathing, a few hours googling her name. And just like every other day, build herself up, minute by minute, then, by 3:30 p.m., no matter how shitty and worthless she might feel, get her ass in gear.

Champagne at Seven!

Every day without fail, and a half-hour before Gwynnie gets home, Olivia forces herself to her feet. She stumbles towards the shower, turns it as cold as she can handle, then reaches for whatever shampoo might be available. Gone were the days of fancy-schmancy products infused with Sicilian citrus, refined mineral water, herbal extracts from some remote village in the Himalayas. Now it's whatever she can scrounge up in the guest bathroom. Over the counter mini shampoos and conditioners—nothing to borrow from her mother, as Gladys had a three time per week hair appointment. "Darling, you know I can't do my own hair!" was what she always said. More like, *she just didn't want to do it herself.*

Afterwards, she'd quickly pull her wet hair back into a ponytail, throw on any remnants of her former wardrobe—she's down to the Ann Taylor Loft dregs, all the good stuff sold off long ago—and force herself to apply a thick layer of concealer and lip-gloss. These used to be Marc Jacobs and YSL, though now she settles for the best and prettiest pink options she can find in Duane Reade's clearance sale section.

Then a few deep breaths, an internal pep-talk, and she plasters on a big, fake smile just as Gwynnie arrives home from her winter break job.

And sometimes, she pulls it off.

At least Gwynnie is doing okay. Better than okay, truthfully, returning every day with stories of the kids she's looking after and the various activities she'd led. Surprisingly, she seemed to love her new job. Gladys was the one who'd suggested it in the first place, only a few days after their arrival, offering up the possibility in her passive-aggressive style. "Oh, it's weeks till school starts . . . you'll be terribly bored, Gwynnie!" She'd said. "That's why parents send their kids to camp! In fact, there's one starting at the Temple, just during winter break. I saw a notice on the Hadassah announcement board looking for counselors . . ."

"OMG, Grandma," Gwynnie had said. "They're hiring and you want me to apply, right? Seriously, life is so much more efficient when you just get to the point, y'know?"

Gladys had raised her eyebrows, surprised. (Clearly, she had not recently had Botox.) Her interactions with Gwynnie had been limited over the years, and this was far from the granddaughter she expected. She'd been shocked to see the tall, practically adult young lady who greeted her at the train station. All that shiny blond hair—the non-Jewish side, Gladys had whispered—but that sharp gaze and the way she spoke her mind. *She's a Kopelman for sure*, Gladys had told Olivia. *Our people have never been afraid to call it like it is!*

"No offense Grandma," Gwynnie had cooed. "And yeah, that sounds kind of cool," She admits with that extra umph of teenage edge. "I'd be a good counselor, I'll bet. Teach those little girls to be empowered, right?" She said, recently becoming enthralled with women's movements. "They should get to know that stuff when they're young. Learn confidence, know their value in society, just like Mika Brzezinski says."

"And what about the little boys?" Gladys had asked teasingly.

"Throw 'em in the corner! LMAO!!!! Just kidding Grandma."

"You'll be a fab counselor," Gladys had pronounced, though Olivia had doubts. She pictured Gwynnie stuck in a room with a bunch of squealing kids, helping them make lumpy Mezuzahs made of clay and having challah food fights at snack time.

She was wrong. Gwynnie loved the job, and every day was a new adventure. "Today I took them on a nature walk and explained global warming," Gwynnie had said a few days earlier. "I mean, I made it simple, but they totally got it. They insisted we start recycling their juice cartons from their snack time! One of them even mentioned all the Neiman Marcus bags his mom had in her closet and asked if they were also recyclable? I was like, yeah! Way to go!"

All in all, Gwynnie was handling this life transition way better than Olivia had. Case in point: at that moment she was curled in a ball, eyes closed, hoping her mother would believe she'd fallen asleep.

"So," said Gladys. "I'm still waiting. This century please. What are your plans?"

Olivia doesn't answer.

"That's right. Exactly my point. You don't have plans. And that, my darling, is the problem." A sigh, and then, with a sudden tidbit of tenderness, "Life is tough, honey. I know. It knocks you flat on your face. That's when you have no other choice. Get up, get moving and make a new one for yourself."

Gladys goes silent, and Olivia hopes that is the end. Daily lesson, finite.

"Did you hear a word I've said, Olivia?" barked Gladys. "Get up and get moving!"

***

Olivia had expected this moment to come. She couldn't live off her mother forever. The house was sprawling, true, and the area exclusive. But just like a lot of her neighbors, appearances could be deceptive. When Milton had died of a heart attack, he'd left Gladys with plenty . . . later, the crash had come, taking a toll on their portfolio. Selling the house would have been a financial loss. Gladys had explained all this a few days after Olivia arrived, not to upset her or cause further agitation, but simply to make her current financial standing clear. "I have plenty to get by, but not enough to support three people forever. I want you here, though, you and Gwynnie . . . I'm so glad you came! Stay for as long as you want. I just needed you to know the reality of the situation. It would break your father's heart if he were around, that I can't just buy you a place, set you up with a new life."

Olivia had never planned to lose touch. Over time, they had begun drifting apart, visits going from frequent to bi-monthly to maybe twice a year; calls from daily to weekly, then to monthly to finally hardly ever. Soon, contact was limited to holiday and birthday cards, the ones for Gwynnie containing a check, of course. Olivia often thought of her mother and would occasionally miss her with a pang so sharp it took her breath away— but the idea of suggesting a get together filled her with anxiety.

It hadn't been a decision, exactly, to cut them off. From their first meeting, Gladys and Edwin had clashed —he found Gladys pushy and overly opinionated, she found him self-centered and obsessed with work. Perhaps they were both right, to an extent, but Milton made up for the tension. Edwin and Milton seemed able to converse well, find common ground—though of a different generation, they were both dedicated businessmen. But then Gwendolyn was born, Edwin grew more successful, and the conversations became strained. Edwin spoke with an unsavory confidence, always boasting with each interaction. Milton appeared less interested, if even slightly bored.

The things Edwin had begun speaking of—his latest account acquisition, his massive campaigns, Fortune 500 clients with houses on both coasts—didn't do much for a man like Milton. The aim was far simpler to him . . . life was not about bragging. He taught Olivia this lesson.

In return, Edwin grew less interested in seeing Olivia's parents. Then Milton had died, and considering his feelings for Gladys, Edwin lost interest entirely. He never said it out loud, but still, his feelings were obvious. "Sure," he'd say to a proposed visit, "but what weekend was that? Don't we have an event?" Or "you know I've got my hands full, Olivia. This new account is killing me . . ." later, he dropped the subtlety. "Do we have to? I have nothing to talk about with your mother."

Sitting in the kitchen, she acknowledged there was another part of the story. But just like everything else, she'd chosen not to pretend it wasn't there. Beneath all that money and standing and admiration, it had all been a beautiful, expensive, and boring lie.

***

Tomorrow, that's what Olivia had told herself every day since returning home. Tomorrow she'd be ready to move forward with her life. She'd get back on her feet, pull herself together, make plans and start again.

A long pause, then the voice . . . quieter than Gladys, but just as familiar, and coming from right next to her on the bed.

"Mom?"

Oh shit. Olivia's eyes snapped open to see . . . Gwynnie, sitting inches away, with an unfamiliar look in her eyes.

Why isn't she at . . . oh yeah. There's no temple camp on weekends. Lunch with the Girls is a Saturday affair. *Duh.*

Concern, that's the look. The one in Gwynnie's eyes.

Olivia shot a look at Gladys, still in the same spot near the door, only now wearing the faintest, self-satisfied twist to her bottom lip. Olivia knows what's going on—Gladys put Gwynnie up to this, no doubt.

"Mom, I'm worried about you," says Gwen. Olivia opens her mouth to object. "No, mom, listen to me. I'm seriously worried, okay? I know what you do all day, too. Pretty much nothing, right?"

Olivia sees no point in objecting; her daughter is too smart. She's also well-adjusted, it seems, at least in comparison to her old lady. Olivia can't believe she is even using that word, *old*, to describe herself. *Wtf!*

***

Unlike Olivia, Gwendolyn had taken the sudden relocation from Georgetown to Jersey with stride. In fact, it had been her idea, and neither Olivia nor her school had put up a fight. Despite having an entire month of spring semester left, the headmaster had been more than happy to comply. *We do understand*, he had concluded, giving Olivia his most understanding look. *You've been through so much. A fresh start is logical. That said, we are terribly sad to see Gwendolyn go. And you too, Mrs. Wyatt.*

Of course they were, Olivia had thought, but not *that* terribly upset. Sad of course, about the loss of tuition, and that Edwin's generous donations were a thing of the past. In actuality, the administration was mostly relieved. By that point, the school knew what was going on, as did everyone else in D.C. . . . and in their minds, Gwendolyn, while much beloved in the school community, was the biggest liability of all.

It was partially the school's fault, whether they liked to admit it or not. For all that money Olivia paid, their security really sucked. How that obnoxious reporter, from a less than savory online outlet, managed to stake out the carpool lane? They had no clue how, with those tall gates and security cameras, the guy had somehow made it through. How he'd staked out the place until the dismissal bell, spotted Gwynnie, and bum rushed her right before the carpool lane. He arrived firing questions like bullets, taking her off guard. *Did she know about her father's secret life? How'd she feel about the turn of events? How about the financial implications, the fact he was living a lie?*

"It doesn't matter," Gwynnie had spit out her answer. "He's not living at all now."

Still, the questions continued, and no one stepped in to help. Not her friends, who'd retreated in horror, nor the mothers who'd watched with both excited and horrified expressions—they'd have plenty to talk about as this gossip was fodder for weeks. Gwynnie was on her own, trying every tactic. Anger, then reasoning, then citing journalistic integrity, her first amendment rights and the fact this so-called "journalist" was a total ass. When that didn't work, she took another tack, threatening to kick him where it hurts, calling him a douchebag and flipping him off. Milton had taught her how to self-defend should she ever need to . . . he always said, *Gwynnie, go right for the balls! And hard!!*

That's precisely when the camera's flash went off. *Click!*

No time for legal action; within an hour, the story made the online gossip rag. By then it was too late, already picked up by other outlets and on the way to global pandemic COVID 19 viral status. It was everywhere, that image of Gwynnie in her school uniform, face screwed up in gorgeous fury for the entire universe to see. Her eyes blazing and middle finger defiantly lifted to the camera. *Wyatt-T-F?* read the New York Post. *Fallen CEO's Hellion Daughter Chip Off Old Block!*

Two modeling agents had emailed Olivia the next day.

"That guy was a total asstard," Gwynnie had explained. "Sorry, Mom. I was mad. But you gotta admit . . . I look kinda cool, right? Kinda punk rock . . . like one of those resistance marchers in the news or those hardcore political activists. Only, y'know . . . cool. And not disenfranchised. But I'm not ashamed, I'm not." Then she sighed. "Though, seriously, Mommy. We need to get outta here. Like, yesterday already. I hate this place!"

As for leaving her life behind, including the school she'd attended from Pre-K onward? If anything, Gwynnie showed relief. "The education is good, sure, but what about the mentality? It's like a cesspool of white privilege. I mean, there are, like, four minorities in the whole place!"

Obviously, she was only counting the black kids—Olivia knew there were at least three Asians, that Hawaiian girl and the one Venezuelan exchange student—but it wasn't a time to argue.

"It'll be good, getting out of here. Maybe we'll even like Jersey, y'know? The shore looks so cool on that one reality show. Hey, what do you know about Snooki?"

Olivia hadn't known what to say, as she was still in a regular state of shock. Maybe this was a natural reaction to their new normal, this laissez-faire attitude. Or maybe, Gwynnie simply just wanted a new start. At the therapist's office—they'd only gone twice, as it was all Olivia could afford—she seemed perplexed. "She appears fine," she had told Olivia after Gwynnie's session. "Despite the upheaval, she appears well-adjusted and mentally healthy. My real concern here, if you don't mind my saying, is not your daughter. I know we have only met briefly, but my real concern, Mrs. Wyatt . . . is you."

"Ms. Kopelman," Olivia snapped. "And I'm not your client, Gwynnie is. Now, would you mind a post-dated check?"

***

Gwynnie and Olivia stare at each other for a moment, silent. "Please, Mom, she says. You've got to do something, okay? Nothing big. Just leave the house! Go to CVS even! Starbucks! McDonald's drive thru. Any-where!"

Olivia doesn't answer.

"I've moved forward with my life, and I'm just a teenager. So, you haven't got an excuse."

"Ok, you're right" Olivia says, heaving herself to sit and putting her feet on the beige carpeted floor. She turns to Gladys, who basks in satisfaction, wishing she could slap that *I win* expression right off her face. "Ok, ok! Can you drive me to the train station, then? I've just decided that I want to go into the city today. Maybe feel out some potential jobs."

"Of course, darling!" her mother chimes, and next to her, she can feel Gwynnie's relief permeate the air.

"About time," Gwynnie says right back, with that all-knowing teenage smirk. "And one more thing!" she says, narrowing her eyes and looking intently at her mother. "Maybe consider putting on some mascara and eyeliner? Maybe a sparkly brown one. And some blush. You are pale as all get out! You can use my stuff—I know you don't have anything. Grandma gave me some money to get a few things at Sephora." She smiles, and Olivia cannot help but laugh. Maybe for the first time in months. "Seriously, though, mom . . . no one wants to hire a hot mess! Get it together . . . you look hideous!"

Chapter Five

07078

Moving to Jersey hadn't exactly been a choice. There was nowhere else to go, and Gwynnie had just fast-forwarded them towards the inevitable. Short Hills, New Jersey.

At that point, it had been two months since that fateful dinner party. A mere two months in which Olivia's perfect and carefully constructed life completely collapsed, leaving behind a pile of debris, transforming Olivia from an upstanding citizen (or so she thought) to broke-ass gossip magnet, society outcast and tabloid fodder.

If only she was being overdramatic.

Soon after the news broke, their private lives spread across newspapers for the world to see. And without pause, the bank's repossession vultures had begun descending. Not just the kind with press passes, either. The kind who arrived with swinging briefcases, waltzing into their townhouse, clipboards ready with scrunched and judgmental eyes. Barely a hello, they began the rotation, stomping across the hardwood floor in ugly, final clearance sale, Designer Shoe Warehouse dated dregs, taking notes and inventory of Olivia's very own life.

Who made this? They'd ask. *Is this a real Rothko? Where did she acquire the Persian carpet, how old is the leather divan, how many rooms were upstairs, and might they use the bathroom, please?* The questions came fast and furious, all the time, their grubby hands reaching out, grabbing for items. Pieces of her former life in strange hands, being contemplated from every angle, turned over and over in their sweaty grasp, making Olivia feel as raw as the oysters she used to eat during summers on Nantucket.

They'd whisper, these people. Confer, consult and nod. They'd eye her with wariness, sympathy and periodic confusion.

"You didn't have an interior designer?" one of them asked, eyebrows raised in surprise. "Well, Mrs. Wyatt, if you don't mind my saying . . . you have excellent taste."

What was she supposed to say? *Thanks? Glad you like my stuff so much, since you plan on taking every bit of it. Assholes!*

Olivia knew the end was near. "It's only a matter of time," Olivia's lawyer warned. "Best to make your arrangements now." *Arrangements,* she thought. Like a death and there was little time to get her final wishes arranged. Forget about sitting shiva. She'll be doing that forever anyway.

Arrangements. Olivia had come to hate that word. Years of arrangements, for galas and fundraisers, for Edwin's funeral. Arranging her home to look perfect, arranging her brain not to see the dark and very dirty truth beneath their perfect address, and socially renowned, enviable lives.

It was all a big fat lie. Every single bit. And the biggest liar of all? Her husband, Edwin Wyatt.

R.I.P.

***

By the time they left, Olivia had sold everything else of value that hadn't been seized, even the car. A quickie exchange with a guy on Craigslist, willing to pay cash—not nearly what the Porsche was worth, but Olivia had been too exhausted to bother haggling. Her designer clothes were gone, her jewelry.

By then, all that remained of their former life—sentimental items mostly—had been driven away and securely locked up in a storage unit just outside the beltway. She'd chosen that place solely for the gratis pickup and offer of *First Month Free!*

Two months and three days after the dinner party, all she physically had were an empty townhouse awaiting auction, a dozen suitcases (she was able to keep two of the LVs at least), and two Amtrak tickets (Mind you the regular slow train now—the Acela days were long over) for the 1:40 p.m. train. And that's what they did, in anticlimactic fashion, without a single tear. There were no goodbye parties or friends to see them off — well, unless you counted Claudia, who'd given them a ride to the station. And she wasn't exactly oozing hopefulness and well-wishes, either. Instead, she spent the entire ride muttering to herself in Spanish and choking back sobs. "Este es terrible! No puedo soportarlo!"

Claudia remained by their side, as the Wyatt family was like her own. But Claudia hated Edwin and did all she could to avoid his very name. Only now and then, when she thought nobody was listening, would she offer up the occasional reference. *El mal hombre*, she'd mutter to herself, adding a hissed, *Que dios guarde su alma!*

***

They had all been there at first, the friends and associates and supporters. Upon learning the news, they had quickly appeared, quick to offer their sympathy-laced help and RSVPs for the funeral. That had been the event of the season, though Olivia barely noticed the enormous crowd, decked out of course in their finest mourning couture, working the scene. The funeral had been *the* sought-after affair, the service so packed that Olivia expected Getty Images to arrive at any moment.

Even following the memorial service, well-wishers continued to appear, members of Olivia and Edwin's circle stopping by the townhouse in the days that followed. They'd arrive at the door, arms loaded down with silver trays of artfully arranged crudites and smoked salmon—this was not *Food TV Sandra's Semi-Homemade* crowd—offering up organic leek and imported French chevre quiches from Patisserie Poupon, alongside their questionably authentic tears. Sympathy gawking, Olivia had begun calling the phenomena, body deflating at each ring of the doorbell. Olivia stayed strong and steadied herself for what was to come—hollow sentiments, squeezed-out tears, subtle digs for information that might be passed along. Corners of eyes being carefully dabbed—those mink eyelash extensions cost a pretty penny, after all—and all those empty words. The visitors would reach for her limp hand, then clutch it in their freshly manicured grip and give dramatic speeches, Olivia staring blankly at their pinched lips with despair, thinking *Who are you, really? I can't believe I ever wasted my time talking to you. What a phony!*

Very quickly, Claudia had gotten the picture, learning the art of makeshift bodyguarding. She would intercede within seconds of the doorbell ringing, reaching for the gourmet trays before they'd even gotten a hello out. "Thank you, missus," she'd chirped. "No, not good time. No today. Maybe later, yes? You call first. Si?"

Wasted breath.

Five days after the funeral, the news officially broke—there was more to Edwin's story than a most powerful life coming to a sudden, tragic and dramatic ending. There were the sides of Edwin few had seen, Olivia included.

It happened that quickly. The first headline, then a rush of them, and instantly everyone disappeared. The Wyatt Enterprises crew, of course—clients, longtime employees, business associates—but that was to be expected. As for the others, their MIA status proved more of a surprise. Overnight, they all were gone—every last one—the carpool mothers and social acquaintances of nearly a decade, the yoga crew and *WTC* sisters and the handful of women she had confided in over the years. Women she had called friends, sharing secrets and reassurances and countless happy hour margaritas. Women who, in the blink of a camera flash, or time it took to write a headline, would no longer be caught dead within a mile of the Wyatt name.

Funny enough, Olivia didn't miss any of these shallow and vulgar deplorables. Not even a bit.

Besides, Olivia and Gwynnie weren't completely alone. There was Claudia, of course, and someone else equally as important—these two people had her back through the thinnest and thickest of bullshit drama. Olivia knew she could count on Daphne; she had been there from the beginning and would stay until the very end. She was the friend who always answered the phone no matter what time of day. She'd bail you out from jail and still lend you money. She'd literally give you the shirt (most likely of silk) off her back. She was one of *those* sort of friends.

This woman, the first to Olivia's side that fated evening of the infamous dinner party from hell. Moments after she opened the front door, only to be greeted by two police officers with stony expressions and slightly lowered heads, Daphne was at her side. Daphne had been the one to catch her, in fact, seconds after she got the news.

Horrible accident. Died on impact.

Strong for an older lady, Olivia remembered thinking abstractly. *Wow! That Pilates after 50-Plus really works!* Then she'd heard the noise, high-pitched and echoing in her ears. Screaming . . . her own.

After that, Olivia remembered little else. Just Daphne whispering reassurances in her ear, a soft pink cashmere scarf muffling shrieks and soaking up tears.

The rage came later that night. Early that morning, really. By then, Olivia had gotten herself together enough to comfort Gwynnie, saying all the right things, stroking her hair as she cried into Olivia's lap. Finally, the girl had fallen asleep, Claudia and Daphne somehow carrying her and getting her upstairs. Only once she was safely out of earshot, fallen into shock-induced slumber, did it really hit Olivia. Not just the pain, like a pickaxe to her gut, but something even more unexpected and violent. Pure, unadulterated rage.

Instantly, Olivia could see the whole scene play out in her head, like a bad movie with a thrown-in twisted ending. There was Edwin, in his non-boardroom business attire—jeans, a crisp white dress shirt, maybe the mahogany-colored alligator-skin shoes as a local flavor homage—getting the tour of the NASCAR facilities. Edwin, basking in the glow of those shiny Skittles rainbow candy-colored machines, taking in the odor of race car fuel and revving motors. An offer had been made, or the subtle suggestion made by Edwin himself—the power of suggestion, that was one of his gifts. Make them think it was their idea the whole time. And like that, he had an open door. Too bad, it was the kind leading to a hulking, dangerous race car.

Edwin couldn't help himself, once the rush of possibility had taken hold. He wasn't thinking clearly, fueled by adrenaline and that mysterious, exotic dirt track. "Wanna take a run?" someone had said, and to Edwin, there was only one answer. She could picture it clearly—Edwin shooting his hosts one of his patented and uber expensive laser-whitened grins, the one that's full of trust and promise and sex appeal with just the hint of mischievous vigor underneath.

"Sure," he'd said offhandedly. "Why not?"

He would be just fine. He was a good driver and had ridden fast vehicles before. Driven a Porsche 120 on the Autobahn, raced the curvy French mountain roads in a Lamborghini. He'd navigated speedboats, helmed ATVs across rough terrains, heli-skied the Alps. Slow down a little? Not Edwin . . . no, nope, no freaking way. Another business trip, another account, another high-risk activity. But a mid-life crisis? He found the very thought ludicrous . . . a decision made by over-the-hill quitters to grow a man-bun, max out their credit cards on some over-priced sports cars pretending that made them relevant.

Champagne at Seven!

As sharply as Olivia could imagine this scene, picture it in razor-sharp detail, the inevitable ending was even more vivid. The slipped hand, the skidding wheel. Screeching tires, bursting flames, billows of sooty gray smoke and machine parts shooting towards the sky . . . parts of Edwin shooting to the sky.

In the following days, Olivia would arrange the funeral, booking the most exclusive funeral parlor in town, and of course secure the Four Seasons for a private reception following. She'd seen to the necessities—of securing a VIP plot in the who's who cemetery of D.C.. When Olivia called to inform Edwin's only living relative of what had happened, she could barely choke out the words once the Boca retirement community had patched her through. "No," Olivia had told Edwin's mother, "you don't understand. It's about your son, Edwin. No, he hasn't dropped out of school, he's grown now. He's . . ."

"Peaches, you say? I cannot accept canned fruit either," expressed his mother.

"But listen now, and I'm sorry, terribly sorry to be the one to share such news. Edwin has passed. Edwin, your son. I realize this is confusing, put the nurse on, will you? No, trust me on this. You ate those butterscotch candies yourself. It happens to the best of us. Now put her on, please. Good, good . . . One last thing.

You do not understand this now, but perhaps you will. If you do have that lucid moment, that clarity, and understand the information I have just given you, please remember this as well. Edwin was a wonderful man who loved you dearly, and you raised him well. You have much to be proud of. Now give the phone to the nurse, please."

But this was long after the funeral, when Olivia had the capability of thought. During those initial days, she couldn't contemplate such things—she could barely dress herself. But she had to motivated and prepare for the service. *I will survive this just fine,* she thought while gently swirling the makeup brush in the Chanel compact, then tap-tap-tapping and applying with precision. She felt broken inside but had to show up. At least for Gwynnie. Olivia decides to go with a muted lipstick, her signature pink, of course, but an appropriate shade. *YSL* in *Rose Saharienne* . . . suggesting elegant-wife-in-mourning vs. chic afternoon at the art museum exhibition followed by cocktails. Finally, and expected, was her LBD. The little black dress that was always her go-to when she didn't know what else to wear. (And, without trying, giving another nod to Coco, the creator of this incredible necessity in every girl's wardrobe—Coco's last-minute creation to attend her lover's funeral. Black of course, being the color of mourning for French widows after the first WW1 slaughter and the Spanish Flu pandemic . . . not to even mention Covid-19). And this certainly was a circumstance where she couldn't even begin to reason on what to wear.

Olivia exited the limo poker-faced, and stayed that way throughout the graveside service, eyes dry behind her black Celine sunglasses. Gwynnie, unlike her mother, mourned appropriately, with tears and whys and understandable confusion. She'd found her mother's zombie state unnerving and worrisome.

Forget Meryl Streep. Olivia deserved an Oscar for this performance. Everyone shot questions to Olivia about what had happened. "We are so sorry! Oh my God, this is terrible!" Olivia was quick to respond. "Tragic, yes. An accident, that's all I will say. A crash, death on impact. Edwin is gone, that's all you need to know. Inquiring into further details is simply bad form on your part, don't you agree?"

The questions would be answered in due time, and in more detail than they could have imagined. Within a week of the burial, the story would leak. Olivia would learn right along with the rest of the world—by watching the evening news. Specifically, Wolf Blitzer's *The Situation Room.*

Tragic accident, yes. But even worse? This was the intentional kind.

The investigation was still pending, but experts on the scene had made their conclusions clear. There was no skidding wheel, no malfunctioning machinery. When he veered towards that wall, Edwin hadn't lost control. He knew exactly where he was headed; he'd picked that direction himself.

Each detail that followed was more alarming than the next. With every blow . . . the fraud, the extra-curriculars, the secrets and deception . . . Olivia felt herself harden. This felt like a story she had read somewhere, a plot on a soap opera, maybe. *No, this cannot be happening to me,* she would think, even as the lawyers began calling. *This is happening to someone else*, she would tell herself, as assets were frozen, seizures put in process.

Her coveted life unraveled as quickly as a ball of the finest Italian cashmere yarn. There were angry people, lots of them, and out for blood. With his untimely end came media interest, with one especially fervent reporter catching wind of the investigation. It had been going on for a year, come to find out. Only a handful of people were aware—FBI agents, IRS investigators, high-level members of the Metropolitan D.C. Police.

Edwin. His lawyers. His Head of Operations, Chad.

It would have all come out soon enough. But instead of waiting for the big public explosion, Edwin chose to go up in one instead.

Edwin was hated, not that he'd ever know six feet under, or even really care if he weren't. He'd stolen a lot of money that wasn't his and lost it—money that belonged to powerful, connected clients. Had Edwin stuck around, there would have been proceedings, a weighing of the evidence. But he was gone now. The information out in public, and directly in the hands of the ferocious media so why put on some pointless show? With his furious former clients pulling strings, the proceedings were put into fast-forward—with Edwin gone, his lawyers had less reason to fight. Edwin had left quite a trail behind—for a sharp businessman, he'd been unexpectedly sloppy.

Perhaps the drugs were to blame.

The drugs for which Edwin and Chad had developed quite a taste were obtained from a well-known drug lord known for serving high-stakes clientele. That's how they learned of Edwin's involvement, from the drug lord's second in command. He'd been arrested and when offered a deal, the feds didn't have to ask twice. He was the one who'd offered names—Edwin Wyatt amongst them—and tipped them off to the pilfered funds. Millions of client dollars tucked away in offshore Swiss and West Antilles accounts, then invested in various sketchy enterprises helmed by less than trustworthy characters . . . those whom Chad had met in his various travels, with whom Edwin regularly socialized, embarking on cocaine-fueled pleasure trips and extravagant jaunts.

So called *business trips.*

The evidence was undeniable; there was a paper trail and there were pictures. Chad posed on deck earlier that year, shirtless, deeply tan, and a crisp white sailor hat perched on his head. How utterly clichéd, Olivia had thought abstractly. His arm slung provocatively over a girl to his left. Hand barely touching the top of her bikini top covered augmented breast. Barely seventeen, that's what the reports said. *Wyatt Enterprises Head of Operations Pulls a Jeffrey Epstein!*

And behind the jailbait, another woman in her early twenties, topless, perched across a man's lap. She whispers in his ear; the man's head is thrown back, mid-laugh. Both hold champagne glasses, and behind, a red-gold sunset glimmers off the waves. The woman was apprehended, and quick to talk—anything not to get extradited back to her country, where she wouldn't last a day. The man? A regular, but unlike Chad, preferred his dalliances with those of legal age.

There was that at least. Small mercy in the big, fucking horrible train wreck of Edwin's immoral and secret life.

Olivia needed to focus inward, specifically on her thoughts . . . *I will overcome any obstacle. I'm digging my heels in and facing everything head on.* Her life would be different now. She realized the future didn't exactly look ideal . . . it looked like New Jersey. She was trading in zip code 20007 for 07078.

Chapter Six

Appearances Can Be Deceiving

This is not Olivia's intended destination. Though, if she was being honest with herself, that was exactly the issue. Olivia has run out of destinations. Her only true haven the past several months has been her bed. She feels out of place already. *I just want to pull the covers over my head,* she thinks. *I have got to get on with things.*

She has no business being in this kind of place. Yet somehow, here she is. Stepping out of the elevator onto the third floor, taking a deep breath and thinking *this feels like home.*

Ten minutes earlier, she'd been standing on the outside of this building, feet firmly planted on the grimy cement sidewalk. She was just passing by, with no intention of even looking into the window, but suddenly she had been drawn like a magnet to the golden lights emanating from inside. Drawn to the crisp shopping bags, the polished and refined shoppers, the stylish sales associates. She had watched them through the door, welding polite smiles and perfume samples, and

thought, *don't they look nice?* It seemed so pleasant beyond that glass entrance. The shoppers serene in the
beauty all around them, and if they so desired, could
take any of it home with them at the right price. A high
price.

This is a happy place, Olivia had thought. Then, her
arm had lifted, seemingly independent of her body, kind
of like when she clutched that champagne flute that horrible evening. Somehow clutching that golden handle,
pushing the door open, and into that oasis, she ended up
inside.

A gush of arctic ice-cold air conditioning, her body
instantly felt lighter, all the ache draining from her
joints. She breathed in the air—fresh and full of new
world assurance—and found herself slowly walking towards the elevator. Once inside, she knew exactly
which button to push. Olivia knew every floor of this
place as well as the rooms in her former Georgetown
townhouse.

Harper James. *The* quintessential department store.
Unlike the consumer conveyor belt of Macy's, or her
favorite and overtly extravagant Harrod's, Harper James
was in a class all to itself. Founded in the 1930's by the
legendary James family—Harper, the patriarch, was
said to be a reclusive genius—the store had always
maintained an aura of exclusivity, just as he had. Like

Saks and Bergdorf's, their reputation had grown over the years, culminating with stores in five cities. Yet Harper James had maintained its old school charm, especially the New York flagship store.

From the vintage tiled ceiling to the Carrara marble counters to the advanced European furniture and decorative accents, this was a place for the discerning client. Only those with the highest caliber of professionalism and industry knowledge would ever be invited to join such an elite staff like the one at Harper James. Olivia was for sure an underdog.

***

Stepping out onto the third floor, Olivia notes the female employees floating in their chic black shift dresses, poker faces of cool competence. A few lift their non-botoxed brows with that unmistakable and even obnoxious question: "how may I help you?" Olivia shakes her head faintly and barely grins. Annoyed, they move on. Unlike other department stores, Harper James employees were never in your face, choosing aloof elegance over the hard pitch. This was true of all the staff, even security—an elderly man in a uniform passed by, offering a polite smile, dapper, in his crisp button down smart coat and badge. Late sixties, perhaps even older, Olivia surmises he has been at Harper James from the beginning, and unlike the rent-a-cops at other department stores, he seems happy with his employment, roaming the floor as one would their own living room.

As she heads towards the back of the third floor, passing through various women's advanced designer areas . . . Prada, Marc Jacobs, Bottega Veneta . . . and navigating the maze of Italian marbled pathways, only pausing when something catches her eye—an Alexander McQueen multi-colored mini-dress, a Givenchy lace-trim nude colored silk blouse—she feels her back growing straighter, her chin lifting—she feels a certain confidence for the first time since her life fell apart. Relishing in this superficial beauty temporarily helps calm her unimaginable anxiety.

She suddenly feels like herself again. Here, in this familiar mecca, she is no longer the notorious widow or ousted socialite; she is just another Madison Avenue woman of means. An average Upper East Side lady who lunches, grabbing a few moments between hot yoga and facial appointments, and secure in the knowledge that, if she dwindles a bit too long, there are maids and nannies waiting to pick up the slack. She snaps back into reality as she continues to roam the store and thinks *no money, no cards, no way.*

After aimlessly wandering along through one room and into another, Olivia suddenly stops dead in her tracks, looking wide-eyed just steps ahead of her. She can't believe her eyes . . . the shimmer beneath the glow of amber lights, rows and rows of them. Like little presents begging to be opened . . . *me . . . me . . . pick me! Me!* They are placed on pedestals, like valued artifacts, or displayed in precise rows with the utmost care. Cognac suede sandals, gold studded black ballet flats, embroidered white lace up booties, azure velvet Mary Janes. And those were just the beginning.

She cradles a single high heeled shoe, holding it up to the light, turning it from side to side, taking in the details. Inhaling the aroma of Italian leather. Crystal-encrusted black mesh, pointed toe, delicate piping. The giddy red sole—Louboutin, of course, offering iconic status, classic appeal and a splash of cool girl attitude. Olivia cups the heel tenderly, taking in the softness and sharp edges, the stiletto, powerfully undeniable, yet delicate as a flower stem. It's like a new love affair for Olivia. Those butterflies and jitters at the start of a new relationship flutter in her gut.

Olivia remembers reading that the brand sells more than 500,000 pairs a year—the red sole an accident in Christian's shoe atelier, Louboutin's assistant's red nail polish became an inspiration for the designer to decorate the normally forgotten plain bottom . . . and now . . . it nets him a huge $100,000,000 in available means. Fashion isn't just fun and beauty, it's a hardcore business.

She feels someone watching her. The department is relatively empty—not that strange for late August, really—except for one other shopper. Young, blonde with obvious dark roots, she shoots Olivia a smile. Olivia returns it, thinking how charitable it is, being around beautiful footwear. How could you be unkind, or cruel, even hateful in the presence of such perfection?

Especially amongst the Louboutins. She gives it a final once over, eyes full of longing. She thinks how once, not long ago, she would have taken the leap. But that was before the credit cards were cut off, the townhouse wiped clean. Before she and Gwynnie boarded a one-way Amtrak train. Regular class.

"Excuse me, Ma'am?" says a voice. Olivia is startled. The young woman is now standing inches away, her overly waxed eyebrows scrunched in concern. "I'm having a total meltdown, you know . . . it's a serious fashion emergency! I need help, if you don't mind . . . like, yesterday."

From one look, Olivia knows this woman inside-out. The designer jeans, the slightly too-long acrylic French nails and the numerous G's on her massive Gucci bag. "I'm Bianca," the woman introduces herself, and beneath the carefully pronounced words, Olivia catches the faint whiff of an accent—the outer-borough kind.

All those years with the *WTC* women, Olivia realizes, had given her one skill. She can read people quickly, with surprising accuracy. The *WTC* women had eyed newcomers up and down, taking quick stock, noting the adequateness, or inadequateness, of every inch. It was more interrogating and intimidating than sorority rush.

Bianca leaned more towards peroxide on the tone scale. Her eyes nervously darted around, as though she was an interloper to these hallowed Harper grounds. She isn't a regular, of that Olivia is sure, and to have made the trek, she had to have had a significant reason. And a subway MetroCard.

Olivia does not have to wonder for long—Bianca immediately launches into her story, happy to overshare. "So, Freddie, that's my boyfriend—he's the best, seriously, it's only been like two months, but it's for real, you know?" Olivia smiles, about to respond, but Bianca doesn't give her the chance. "So, like, he's the real deal. Good family, hardcore job." She leans in, lowers her voice. "Wall Street!" Olivia nods, unsure of why this woman has chosen to tell intimate details to a random Harper James has-been shopper but doesn't want to appear rude. "So, I'm going to meet his family," she says, voice suddenly edged with fear. "And I found this great *VERSACE* dress—costs a fortune, but Freddie paid. He's really thoughtful like that. But I don't have any idea what shoes to wear, you know?" Bianca leans in closely, voice low. "Can I be honest?"

"Of course," says Olivia.

"The other women here are kind of, you know, how do I say this? Uptight and cold. And you, you're different. I don't know, but gut instinct tells me you are really authentic."

That's when Olivia realizes. She glances down at her outfit, a dress she had found in the back of Gladys's closet. Ancient, but beautifully constructed, and timeless enough it could pass as brand new. As to the brand, she hadn't looked at the tag, but it was a simple shift. Black, of course. It would do just fine. And, she had no other option.

She looked just like a Harper James employee.

A quick scan of the area, and Olivia spots a real employee. Two shoe displays away and behind a counter, the saleswoman appears occupied by a computer—she stares at the screen, as though going over inventory, though Olivia suspects she is hiding a cell phone. Texting, probably, or scrolling through Instagram. The woman makes no effort to assist and has also most likely deemed Bianca a low priority—i.e. from an undesirable demographical zip code and lacking in spending power.

Never profile a customer. Appearances can be deceiving.

Olivia opens her mouth, ready to tell the truth. She was shopping, just like Bianca, with only one difference. Unlike the eager young woman before her, there was no "Freddie" to pay the bill. In fact, Olivia had nothing specific to shop for anymore, literally. Not even a *WTC* event which she hated anyway.

***

It had only been a week earlier that Gwynnie sat on the edge of her bed, face wracked with concern. Olivia had finally heaved herself to sitting, then ultimately to her feet, leg muscles trembling.

She contemplated washing her hair.

Olivia might *feel* like a hot mess, but she needn't look that way. "Yes, take me to the train station," she'd told Gladys. "But can I have an hour first?" Gladys had nodded, glowing at having gotten her way, and watched Olivia slowly making her way to the bathroom, smug as could be.

Slowly stepping into the bathroom, Olivia turned on the light and looked closely in the vanity mirror. She let out a deep exhale. *At least this once*, she thought, *may as well properly bathe—no 15 second rinse off this time.* Enjoying the steaming hot water, she stood underneath with her eyes closed, trying to focus and stay in the moment, finally taking a break from hours of cable network news repeat headlines and *90 Day Fiancé* marathons on *TLC*. Olivia soaped every inch, and shaved her legs— oh, how she missed the waxing appointments—and finally, washed her hair. And not with generic drug store shampoo, either, but with an expensive European product she found hiding behind a stack of towels in the linen closet. *Finally, and how long has this been there?* she thought. She'd generously lathered, rinsed, and done it again. Just because. This was the closest she'd come to luxe anything since she could recently remember. By the time she was finished, she was sparkling, every strand on her head squeaky clean. At last.

She'd blow-dried carefully, then styled and carefully applied her makeup all while endlessly staring into her closet, contemplating the limited resources. Why had she been so quick to sell all her good stuff? What was left were the dregs of a once enviable closet, drugstore makeup, shabby t-shirts, and three old designer handbags from 2018. Now considered vintage.

After much contemplation, Olivia had chosen the best and most professional options available, as sad as they were—a grey *Ann Taylor* skirt and an ordinary white blouse. *When in the hell and WHY did I buy these? Borrrrrring*, for sure, but she had to admit it felt good finally taking off the sweats. Olivia was dressed and ready to go. The question was, where was she going and what was her plan? How she wished Daphne was with her. Olivia knew Daphne would be the best person to help her now. She reached for her cell and quickly dialed.

Shit, voice mail. "Daphne, hi, it's Olivia. I'm sorry I missed you. I'm . . . I'm just thinking of you and missing you so much. I'm going into the city and just wanted to hear your voice. Ask you what I should do next? I have so many thoughts swirling in my mind that I'm nauseous. Ok, I will try you later. Love and miss you. Bye."

Half an hour later, after her mother had driven her to the station, Olivia boarded a regular commuter train to New York City, her future uncertain. Settling in her seat, she looked around and out the window. Taking a deep breath, she assured herself everything would be ok. As the train rushed forward, another rush of worry; in response, Olivia closed her eyes, again, and tried to settle her mind. She went to the café car for a white wine, something to help calm her nerves. With the $100 bill Gladys gave her, Olivia considered the drink a necessity and decided to give up overpriced coffee in exchange.

I've had enough caffeine already and I have got to calm down. She sipped the wine and pondered.

Olivia would prove herself, that was the only choice. She would start over, she vowed, ending up with a life better than before. That couldn't be that hard, right? Anything was better than being married to a lying, cheating, embezzling fraud. Living in a house, and life, paid for and built on lies.

Forty minutes later, standing on the escalator elevating her up into Penn Station, Olivia realized how lucky she had been. How she never had to worry about money. About bills. After all those years in her more than comfortable Georgetown existence, she had forgotten about . . . all this . . . real life. They had visited New York, of course, Gwynnie, Wyatt and Olivia, but these had been trips of the five-star hotel, chauffeured variety. Now she was smack in the midst of it and there was nothing luxurious at all. She had stood there, amidst the chaos, the noise and foul aromas, fighting the urge to buy a one-way return ticket and head right back to Short Hills. She breathed in deeply. Breathing in everything she had been so carefully shielded from in life. The harshness of reality.

She steadied herself, looked forward and went plunging into the crowd. She stayed laser focused on finding the exit, trying to tune out the booming loudspeakers and distractions. She weaved through bodies, ignored catcalling teenagers, dodged cops arguing with homeless men and tourists bickering over maps. She stepped aside as a sudden rush of three-piece suits exited the subway in mass man-stride—had she not, these bastards would probably have steamrolled right over her with their Chateau Margaux bloated egos and $900 exotic skinned shoes. *Move forward*, she'd thought, and had done just that, blocking everything else out. She'd jumped off the escalator, eyes focused on the exit above, pretending she hadn't just seen a guy pee right next to the Wetzel's Pretzel stand. What a stark contrast to her previous life.

Finally, she arrived, exhausted. *To the street.*

Olivia rushed through the doors, leaving the stench of sweat, urine and trash behind, only to be greeted by . . . honking, the smell of gasoline, hot dogs and even more bodies than there were inside. Still, the sun was shining, the buildings towering, sun glittering off the endless windows from above. She took a deep breath, filling her lungs with sooty air and felt her spirits rise. Though she hadn't been here in years—it felt just the same, the bustling metropolitan city—full of unexpected surprises. New York City, where everything was possible. She was on the hunt. This time not for anything designer and superficial. This time it would be for her stability. Her new life.

Olivia had moved quickly to protect her daughter, and then of course appeased her mother, but perhaps she should have planned better. She might have acted too quickly. She had come in search of a job, but . . . what kind? And where? She couldn't even remember which way was uptown, let alone find the direction she was headed in her life now? No such thing as a humanity and survival compass.

***

Olivia had spent the next five hours wandering the city, mind scattered in a million directions. She needed to find a job. She had walked block after block, and at some point, found herself thinking of when she was a kid spending time with her mother, Gladys, who never had an "official" job, or at least an authentic one. Rather, she shopped and viewed her shopping trips with the seriousness of a proven career. And often, in Olivia's younger years, instead of her mother getting a babysitter, she just came along.

She'd follow at her mom's Chanel heels to many locales, as varied as the selections they offered. There were ordinary stores in the mall, and discount dives where women changed in one large fitting room, seemingly unembarrassed by the layers of flab or saggy arms. Then there were the hidden, expensive boutiques, and trips to the city, where they would visit the higher-end establishments. Places that were quiet and with air conditioning as cold as North Pole temps.

Places like Harper James.

Wherever they ended up, Olivia would carefully observe her mother as she perused racks, seeking some elusive quality she called *well-made*. Gladys would disregard pieces much more quickly than accepting them, but once they had passed her internal test, she immediately scouted out the nearest employee, waiting to be escorted towards the dressing room. That was Olivia's favorite part, watching her try on the clothes. She would sit, quietly fascinated, observing as her mother zipped, snapped, adjusted, turned from side to side and assessed. The same happened at home, as new pieces were combined with the old in unexpected ways. Olivia learned one of her early style lessons: old wasn't always old. With just the right sleight of hand, you could reinvent it into something new, allowing the world to experience it in an entirely fresh light.

Olivia had tried this for herself early on, to mixed results. "She can't wear that!" Her mother would squeal, taking in her newest preschool creation of mint green turtleneck, shiny lavender plaid tights and orange tutu. "They'll call Social Services!" Her father would shrug. "Let it go," he'd say, waving Gladys off, then turning to Olivia with a wink. "I think she looks fabulous. A real stylist, my little girl!"

Olivia had grinned widely, skipping happily towards the door, comfortable in the knowledge she looked just right. Even as a mere child, fashion felt natural, and she knew clothes should reflect who she was inside—at that moment, at least. Some days, she felt like fluffy layers of purple and poof, other days, a grungy old tee with her fancy high holiday skirt. Her father stepped in enough that Gladys finally gave up, and Olivia was free to wear anything she desired, however odd it may have been.

She continued to experiment, but her choices grew more refined, her fashion-forward leaps more thought-out. As a preteen and teen, she never went with the crowd, buying into fads like many of her friends. "Acid washed jeans?" Just looking at them hurt her eyes. Grunge was just like it sounded, ugly, and jelly belonged on bread, not on your feet or shoulders. Instead of following trends, she went with her heart, following fashion impulses that might come on a sudden interest or whim. When they studied flappers in middle school, she'd worn drop-waisted shifts and faux pin curled hair for a week; later, after catching a Bardot flick on late night TV, she'd gone through a mini, lip-sticked-pout-and-teased hair phase. English new wave, classic Madonna, punk rock, Olivia had dabbled in them all. However crazy or unexpected or off-trend, one point all could agree; Olivia had great taste.

She was the one friend you needed when shopping for a dress before a dance; whose honest outfit critique and feedback was most often sought. When she'd convinced her parents to send her to boarding school the only drawback had been the uniforms. Convincing her parents of the relocation had been a long process, but well worth the effort—she argued it was only a few hours away. But beyond required plaid skirts, Peter Pan collared blouses and shit-colored cardigans? For a second, she wondered if she'd made a mistake.

Still, Olivia had made the best of the situation, integrating style into her new school life. There had been frequent dress up parties in her dorm room, where the girls would break out their civilian clothes, letting Olivia help guide unexpected ensembles. Once prettied up, heels and all, they'd gather their filched and top-secret resources—cheap champagne, the occasional pint of whiskey or vodka minis, and commence with a dorm room cocktail party. Lights off, of course. Music volume up. The other main concern was getting expelled, though that was never an actual option. *Milton would kick my ass!*

By the time she entered college, Olivia had ceased the overt experimentation, finding her own look—sophisticated, with unexpected dashes of rock and roll, not afraid to draw attention but never boastful. By then, Olivia had concluded, and embraced it as eternal truth: *just the right outfit can change your entire life.* Just by the choice of fabric, texture, color and style, you could do anything—lift your spirit, compliment your surroundings, exude sex appeal and mystery, own the room and feel perfectly on top of the world. Look at J. Lo and Elizabeth Hurley in *Versace*! It really put them both on the map, and amped up their careers. Just by wearing the right dress.

As for fashion as a career choice, that never occurred to Olivia, not even with her foray into the retail sales world. The work had been an accident—the summer following her first year of college, Olivia didn't *need* to get a job, by any means. Like so many of her peers in their upper-crust suburbs, her parents were more than willing to support her. Milton and Gladys had the money, and after those years of boarding school, a limitless credit card was a small price to pay for having her home again.

Unfortunately, New Jersey was the last place she wanted to be, black card or not.

Olivia's friends were away on vacation or had stayed near their own universities. They were on summer abroad programs, or had taken internships—*why hadn't she thought of that?* Instead, Olivia had made no plans despite the pressure from her parents to get a summer job.

Within a week, Olivia had set her mind to finding one, and she didn't care what kind. She couldn't take her parent's nagging anymore about finding a job. Retail seemed like the natural option, so the Ellen Rossdale boutique had been the first place she approached. Olivia couldn't imagine days spent at a mall, frequenting the food court between folding binges at the Gap. Ellen Rossdale was in an upscale shopping "destination," an outdoor development frequented by mom types, and that seemed okay—while she didn't care for the piped in muzak, she figured it was better than helping whiny Jersey teenagers looking for *just* the right tank.

As for Ellen Rossdale, they jumped at the chance, offering Olivia a position on the spot. The manager, Pippie, was more than happy to employ such a lovely and young woman amongst their mostly middle-aged—aka antiquated and incredibly unhip—staff. A staple of the elderly WASP set, Ellen Rossdale was for those old money wannabes who aspired to summer in the Hamptons but ended up in an Atlantic City two week AirBnb. To the Lilly Pulitzer wannabes, the aesthetics were frills, poufs, princess cut skirts and their signature flower-and-vine patterned shopping bags, logoed wallpaper and in-store carpet. Not Olivia's taste, for sure, but she had selling in her blood, she reasoned.

What she never expected? In the first month, she outsold all the other employees. Beginners streak, maybe, until she did it again. And again. No one had been more surprised than Olivia herself. Somehow, without putting in any effort, she had demonstrated all the right skills.

All those years poring over fashion magazines had given Olivia the right turn of phrase, and she'd had plenty of experience as a makeshift wardrobe consultant for friends. Ellen Rossdale was simply an extension of that, only for paying customers. She naturally had a knack for picking just the right pieces to meet the client's needs. And let's not forget body types. That, along with the strategically placed accessory, she had somehow replaced Ellen Rossdale's notorious frou-frou factor with the wunderbar-wow kind. As for her sales techniques, there wasn't much beyond natural enthusiasm, charm and knowing her audience.

"Easy and fun," she would tell the young shoppers—youngish, as the clientele was at least 40 plus, but she knew the Ellen Rossdale true devotees, and could spot a rich woman with bohemian longings a mile off. "You look like a summer breeze," she would tell them in a gush. "And just picture it on the beach, with bare feet, even a floaty tunic!" To the matrons, speak with polite deference, and use the words "classic" and "youthful" a lot. "The hemline is demure," she would explain, "yet elegant. A classic silhouette, yet also somewhat youthful to highlight your fun personality . . . and look at your waist! I can only hope at your age I look half as fab. How do you do it?"

Two summers she worked at Ellen Rossdale, breaking sales records each time. Then, right before her senior year in college, she had been scouted by a regular customer—a fashion consultant—for an assistant position. A local stylist, the woman mainly did local photo shoots, but she'd leaned on Olivia, valuing her insight and wardrobe suggestions. Whether a local car dealership spot or shoe store ad, Olivia had been involved in every step of the process, from selecting models to styling the sets to hair and makeup. Olivia had enjoyed the job, just as she had the one at Ellen Rossdale, mainly for the gift of helping women transform themselves. She loved to make suggestions they'd never expect, ease them into giving it a go, then watching faces light up as they scrutinized their new reflection, smiling like peacocks who had only just discovered they had feathers, let alone such magnificent ones.

***

Olivia remembered the fated evening, and the words her dear friend shared. "You have your whole life," Daphne had said.

Just like that, she'd made the decision. One that didn't involve pleasing anyone but herself. Sure, it was crazy, probably deluded . . . but she could try, right? It wasn't too late.

In fact, it was just the beginning.

She could start in high-end retail, work her way up the chain. Or maybe styling, merchandising, window visuals, that kind of thing. It would come naturally, she told herself. She had experience. Even more, she had good instincts. And, no Ivy League school could teach instinct, that's for certain.

She had taken the train back to Jersey with a feeling she hadn't experienced in a while—*hope*—and a mission to set out the next day fully prepared. That night, she had put together a killer outfit, going so far as to raid her mother's closet. Vintage chic, she told herself, then sat down and typed up a resume, highlighting the retail experiences and making the employment dates a smaller font. Who cared about dates anyway? Experience is experience. Besides, she was willing to start at the bottom. She had no choice but to put in the sweat and tears to prove herself. Yet once again.

For the next week, Olivia had woken up every day with a newfound sense of determination. She had started on the high-end of the scale, working the boutiques on the Upper East Side, taking a deep breath before striding into each store. "I'm here to inquire about a job," she would tell the sales associate, voice confident. "Whom might I speak with?" Turns out, it couldn't have mattered less. She could talk her throat raw, and she'd be no closer to a job.

***

Now, another week later, she is still nowhere near landing a fashion job, yet she's inadvertently fallen into acting the part. Bianca talks and talks. Diarrhea of the mouth really. Olivia does nothing to stop her. "Le Bernardin," she babbles. "Freddie's parents love the place. Never been there myself, but it's fancy-shmancy I hear. I'm more of a hamburger or spaghetti and meatballs kind of girl, I just love Maggiano's you know, but anyway, I want to look . . . you know . . . sophisticated . . . elegant . . . so what kind of shoes go with a black Versace dress? I mean, it's fitted at the waist, and . . ."

Olivia, watching her mouth move, is dumbstruck. For the past week, all she has heard is *no*, and for positions far less prestigious than Harper James. After all that, this girl—Bianca—believes her to be an employee.

After countless dismissals, curt rejections, pandering gazes and excuses, after hearing *we-aren't-hiring-for-the-time-being-we'll-keep-you-in-mind-you-just-aren't-quite-the-right-fit-so-sorry (i.e., You're too old!)* After all that rejection, this random stranger, Bianca, does not question Olivia's persona at one of the most prestigious retail establishments in the western world.

"Um, well, you don't have much experience," one woman had said, though "woman" was a subjective term. A manager at Zara, Lydia hadn't looked a day over fifteen, and the braces were just part of it. That had been only a few hours earlier, and a last-ditch effort; at that point, Olivia had tried more places than she could count, from high to low, upper east to lower west. Going into Zara in a bland midtown mall. A final act of desperation. And in response, a pudgy-faced manager with a half-fixed overbite and eye rolling habit had stared at her resume with disdain. "So, you do have experience?" she asked to which Olivia had pointed out

Ellen Rossdale and her brief styling gig. "Yeah, but those were like, years and years and years ago?" She said in that upspeak Olivia hated, like the verbal equivalent to nails on a chalkboard. "Like, our demographic is more . . . current? You get it, right? You know what I'm saying? You just seem more mature than our clients. And the sales team too. I just don't think you would be a good fit here."

Women of Olivia's age didn't embark on retail jobs, they were already in them, hopefully having risen far above the ranks of steaming garments, folding, and organizing racks. Women Olivia's age didn't get to work their way up the ladder; in fact, they never even got close to the first rung. Her time was up, her day had passed, and starting over? That had been a fantasy in her head.

Olivia is startled from her musings, suddenly remembering the girl in front of her. The one who has gone from eager, nervous babble, to staring at her with wide, hopeful eyes. Bianca, meeting the love of her life, Freddie, who not only finds him a breath of fresh air but sees them together for life. Only issue? The uppity Upper East Siders who spawned him and hoped for the appropriate match. They saw him with a Rothschild heir, not a next of kin to a Long Island used car dealership or neighborhood pizza parlor business. Everything rested on this upcoming dinner, and to Bianca, her success rested on looking the part. But still, something was missing . . .

"I have a picture on my phone. Of the dress. Maybe if you see it, you'll know the right kind of shoe?"

"Yes, absolutely," says Olivia firmly, lips lifting into a pleasant smile. "Once I know what we're working with, I'll know exactly where to start."

Olivia weaves her way through the displays, Bianca hot on her tail, making quick, strategic selections—Oscar De La Renta pointed-toe with intricate beading, a Gucci stiletto with pearl-encrusted bow. "Ooooh!" squeals Bianca with each selection, "These are gorge!" She only hesitates when handed a jeweled Manolo. "I mean, I love it, don't get me wrong, I love all of them, but are they too . . ."

"Absolutely not," says Olivia with a comforting smile. "The dress is very chic, perfect for the occasion. But why not bring in a little bling too? That's your style, right?" Bianca gives a worried nod. Olivia understands—she loves the shoes, the same way she loves her rhinestone-tipped acrylic nails. She is outspoken, fun. The kind of girl who livens up the room, isn't afraid of a dirty joke and never hesitates to be the first on the dance floor. She was born with flash and glittered confidence.

But Freddie's parents? They might not be the glitter-embracing type.

Bianca stares down at the shoe, running her fingers along the crystal-encrusted brooch at the front. She is at a crossroads. Olivia knows how that feels and can also see "it" clearly, what Bianca is about to face. Sure, Freddie might be great, but his parents won't be so easily won over. She can look the part, decking herself out in ready-to-wear, a fancy updo and Chanel Number 22 perfume (Olivia's personal favorite of the *Les Exclusifs* collection,) but they won't notice any of it. They won't see her vivaciousness, or natural intelligence, or how much she loves their son—all they will see, and hear, is Staten Island.

"Never lose who you are," says Olivia, with a quick pat on her shoulder. "Not for anyone. That sparkle is what Freddie fell in love with, after all. That's who you are."

Instantly, Bianca seems to grow taller, a flush of confidence on her face. She grins at Olivia. "You're right," she says, not bothering to hide the accent. "I love these shoes."

"Eh hem." The clearing of a throat, and both women turn. The saleswoman, who has torn herself from Instagram, is now staring at them with curiosity and a tight smile. "Did you want to try those on?"

Bianca looks confused, glancing from Olivia to the saleswoman and back again. Her eyes narrow. "Wait," she says to Olivia. "You don't work here, do you?"

Olivia shrugs and smiles. Bianca breaks into a peal of laughter.

"That," she says. "Is effing hilarious!"

Her smile pulled to the uncomfortable breaking point; the sales associate practically steps between them. "No, she does not. But I would be happy to help you."

Now she wants to help, thinks Olivia. One customer in a deserted department, and it took her this long to get off her ass? Olivia hadn't been into the Harper James flagship in years, but she was shocked how the customer service had declined.

"Oh yeah?" questions Bianca. "So now you wanna help me, huh?"

"Of course!" says the woman, glancing nervously towards the aisle. "It's my job!"

"Coulda fooled me," says Bianca.

The woman turns quickly, plucking a shoe from each of Olivia's hands. Despite the smile, Olivia can see the panic in her eyes. "Now, these are floor models. And they must be handled carefully, as they are very expensive." She whips around, her back to Olivia. "So, tell me what you're looking for, and we can . . ."

"I like those," says Bianca, not trying to hide the accent anymore. Hands on her hips, freshly waxed chin defiantly lifted, she stares down the woman. "Expensive, huh? What are you implying?"

"I wasn't implying anything! I just meant those are our high-end brands and . . ."

"Well, good thing I'm not paying, then," says Bianca, pulling a black card from her black leather Dior wallet and thrusting it towards the woman. "My boyfriend is . . . and yeah, feel free to call and verify. His name is Eddie Lelliman. He works on Wall Street."

Lelliman. Olivia almost laughs. Lelliman Skytrade, a top firm. Once, in her former life, her late husband had mentioned Edward Lelliman, calling him a legend. And Eddie must be the Junior.

"May I be of some service, ladies?"

"Hello, ladies." The voice is not loud, but commands attention. The three turn to the aisle, where a tall, elegant man observes them. Next to Olivia, the saleswoman visibly stiffens. "Oh, Mr. DuPaul! We were just . . ."

She does not finish her sentence; the man is already striding towards them. He is tall and thin, with glossy black hair, high cheekbones and an impeccably well-fitting suit. Brioni? Canali? Zilli even? No, this is bespoke, made just for him. Saville Road, perhaps, and the style, old-school—checked virgin or merino wool, notch lapel—giving him the air of having come from another era. Not handsome, exactly, but debonair, aristocratic. *Important.*

"Ladies," he says, giving Olivia and Bianca a smile with his perfectly white teeth. Unnaturally white, in a way not achieved with gels or lasers. Lumineers? Back in the day, Olivia would have asked for a referral to his cosmetic dentist.

"Mr. DuPaul! So nice to see you," chirps the saleswoman, and the man contemplates her, face unreadable. "I was just helping this lovely woman to . . ."

"Helping," snorts Bianca.

The tiniest flicker of Mr. DuPaul's eyebrow, and that's when Olivia understands—not only is this guy a superior, but he's also a big time superior. His arrival, in fact, is probably the reason this employee went from sexting or Instagramming or whatever she deemed more important than a potential client, to rushing over and offering breathless assistance, panic stricken. Unfortunately for her, he was passing by, maybe.

Judging from her face, she never expected him to stick around.

"So, tell me," says the associate to Bianca. "What size did you say you wanted?"

"I didn't say. You never asked me."

The saleswoman opens her mouth, but too late as DuPaul has already turned towards Bianca with a warm smile; she smiles back, basking in the glow of his attention. Suddenly, the Harper James employee seems to fade away and good riddance; this guy is town and country charm personified.

"I'm sorry, we haven't been formally introduced," he says, voice rich. He extends a long-fingered hand, and even his nails are groomed to perfection. "I'm Felix DuPaul, and you are?"

He looks at her like she is the only girl in the world, Bianca practically melting. "Bianca Rossi," she says with a giggle.

"And, Bianca, to what do we owe the pleasure of your visit to Harper James?"

Moments later, Bianca is situated comfortably in a chair, a stack of shoe boxes beside her. She gazes down at her feet, rapturous, then sucks in her breath and stands.

The Manolos. The BBs. The option Olivia advocated for.

Instantly, Bianca is transformed. She stands taller and not just from the heels. With a sweep of his arm, Felix guides her to the closest mirror, and Olivia stands back, watching Bianca's confident stride, lifted and augmented size DD chest and slightly raised botulinum toxin in-need brow. She consults her reflection, almost regal.

"Are you effing kidding me?" squeals Bianca. "These are stunning! Breathtaking!"

Almost.

"What do you think?" she asks Mr. DuPaul. A split-second, as he contemplates her feet, finger to chin. "Divine," he says to which Bianca squeals again, this time sounding more like the star of the new *Debbie Does Dallas*.

"I know, right? When Olivia picked them, I was like, are these too much? But she was totally right! I mean, Eddie is going to freak. He's really into shoes, you know. I mean, don't get me wrong, not in a freaky way. He's not one of those feet pervs or anything," she says, giggling. Mr. DuPaul nods, giving her a slightly amused smile. "He's more of a butt guy, to tell you the truth, but he has all these Italian loafers that cost a fortune and he's always saying I should treat myself and you get what you pay for, so when . . ."

Just like that, Olivia snaps back to reality, remembering who and where she is. *This has been fun*, she thinks, *but what's the point?* Here she is, in a store where she can't afford a thing, her bag full of unwanted resumes, her life still in shambles and a 5:30 LIRR train to make.

Bianca is occupied; no point in saying goodbye. As much as she loves the glossy, golden-lit Harper James cocoon, she can't avoid the grimy, gray and real world for very long. Her new reality.

Olivia sighs, turns and heads for the elevator.

***

"Excuse me?"

Olivia is staring at her gilded reflection in the third-floor elevator, dreading the upcoming descent and exit from this peaceful shopping enclave—when the voice interrupts. She knows who it is before even turning. Rich, resonant and unmistakable.

Felix DuPaul.

Shit. What did she do now? Break some rule by pretending to be a sales associate? Or maybe this man simply senses, like everyone else in the world now, that she does not belong. That Olivia is a disgraced woman. The kind who comes into the legendary Harper James without the means to make a purchase, simply there to cause disruption.

A deep breath, and she turns.

"Olivia, was it? We haven't been formally introduced."

Mr. DuPaul contemplates her with his inscrutable expression and seemingly poreless skin. He could be anywhere from thirty to fifty-six, this man. Faintly European, his air, but who knows? Iowa farm boy, Upper East Side snob, it doesn't really matter. He gives her a once over, almost imperceptible. A flicker of the eyes, not even a millisecond, taking her in from slightly scuffed pumps to disheveled chignon. Olivia knows what he is seeing; this isn't her first shopping rodeo.

"Are you a Harper James regular?"

"As a matter of fact, I am."

"Indeed," says Mr. DuPaul. "I see."

Two words, but the dismissiveness cuts like a knife. Olivia knows exactly what he sees. She lifts her chin defiantly, staring him dead on.

"Or I used to be. I haven't come by in a while, if you want to know the truth. And to be quite honest, I'm surprised by how much everything has changed."

"Oh, yes? Please elaborate, Ms . . ."

"You can call me Olivia. And Harper James is renowned for their customer service, but that poor girl, Bianca . . . well, she was desperate for help. The place was practically empty, and your employee was completely ignoring her. Until she spotted you, I suspect. And even after running over, she was, how shall I put this? A tad dismissive." Olivia feels the rage rising in her. Right then, Felix Du Paul is every person who has turned her down this past week, dismissing *her*. He is the boutique manager who thinks she is unqualified, the Zara employee who thinks she is too old. He is every judgmental, entitled asshole in this entire godforsaken city who won't give her a chance to even fill out an application.

Felix stares at her, and that's when Olivia realizes. She isn't required to stand here or talk to this man. She hits the elevator button, and like a miracle, the door whooshes open. Olivia steps inside. "This place has really gone downhill," she mutters.

Felix reaches out, stopping the door just in time.

"You are exactly right, Ms. Wyatt," he says.

Wait. How does he know my name?

He dips his head slightly, voice low. "I am terribly sorry for your loss." Before she can speak, he does. "Perhaps, I might interest you in a cup of tea?"

They are on a floor Olivia has never seen, high above the brightly lit consumer paradise, where the sterile, gray carpeted hallway is lined with offices. Yet here, in the expansive corner unit, Olivia has entered an alternate world. Antique Tabriz carpet, carved oak bookcase and immense windows overlooking a bustling Fifth Avenue. Even with the massive mahogany desk, 19th Century Regency, the room feels less like a workplace and more like a Victorian parlor. A little old fashioned for her taste, but Olivia can't help but be impressed—this man has style, no doubt.

I need to get out of here. Olivia feels as raw as an open wound.

Mr. Du Paul disappears for a moment, arriving with a tray. She watches as he arranges a cup and saucer in front of her, his every movement deliberate, yet refined. "Would she prefer Chamomile or English Breakfast? Perhaps the Moroccan Pomegranate?" Olivia tells him that sounds fine, though, by this point, she would prefer a couple shots of whiskey instead. "Sugar? One cube or two? Lemon?" Olivia agrees to everything, feeling utterly out of place.

Finally, they sit across from each other. Felix contemplates Olivia, as though waiting for something. She takes a sip.

"Lovely china," she says. "Royal Copenhagen? And, um, how do you know who I am?"

"Oh," says Mr. DuPaul. "Society pages, perhaps."

Right. In the aftermath of her husband's demise, and the unfortunate avalanche of news that followed, Olivia has been careful to avoid those succubus interlopers with their cameras. Still, there had been a few unfortunate snaps, catching her unbeknownst. Even disguised in sunglasses and scarf—very Jackie O, she had thought at the time, sans the dignity—you could still recognize her drawn, agonized face. If you were looking hard, that is, or read the gossip columns of third-tier publications.

"You know it is my job to keep up on these things," says Mr. DuPaul, as though privy to her very thoughts. "Society goings-on, that sort of thing. Our clientele is elite here at Harper James, so keeping abreast of the social scene is of the utmost importance."

He takes a sip of tea, contemplating Olivia, his face passive, unreadable.

"And I must admit, your story stood out. I feel sympathy for what you have experienced, Ms. Wyatt."

Beneath DuPaul's refined façade, Olivia thinks she sees something familiar—the vaguest tinge of smug curiosity, of judgment-laced assessment. She knows how to spot the signs and can sense what people might be thinking about her. She has experience, after all. Decades of it. Gold digging trophy wife or white-collar widow, either way, she knows when she is simply a circus act. *That's why I must be here*, Olivia decides. *To break up this guy's day, to give him fodder for his next lunch at the Yale Club. You'll never believe who I met!* That's what he'll say. She can just imagine him knocking back a second martini, launching into the story. Serving juicy details, taking his sweet time. *So, I'm*

*walking the third floor, and guess who I spot making a
scene? Remember that Edwin Wyatt story? Well . . .*

Who does this guy think he is?

"Well," she says abruptly, reaching for her bag.
"Thanks for the tea, but I have a train to catch."

"Ms. Wyatt, I hope I haven't offended you."

"It's Kopelman now. And . . . offended? I'm way
past that, Mr. DuPaul. Let's just be honest here, can we?
I'm not exactly part of your elite clientele, at least not
anymore. Then again, I hate to say it, but this place isn't
quite what it used to be either." Olivia stands. "I used
to frequent this establishment, believe it or not."

"Wait," he says, rising to his feet. "You misunder-
stood me!"

"I mean, the customer service is now deplorable. I
stepped in today to help that poor girl because no one
else would. And now I have a train to make." At the
door, Olivia sighs. "I hate to tell you this, Mr. DuPaul,
but this place has really gone downhill. Thanks again
for the tea. You're right, the Moroccan Pomegranate
was very good."

Olivia turns.

"You are exactly right," says Mr. DuPaul, stopping
her in her tracks. "Not about how I view you, but about
the store. In fact, that is the reason I invited you up
here."

Two hours later, Olivia sits in a crammed train car, mind racing as fast as the New Jersey transit. Next to her, a sweaty and middle-aged guy manspreads, hogging the arm rest and cramming her against the window as he reads the New York Post.

Olivia hardly notices. What just happened?

Mr. DuPaul is what happened. "Call me Felix, please," he had said, "and may I call you Olivia?" He had beckoned her to sit again, poured more tea and, voice measured, calmly agreed with her assessment of the store. Harper James had undoubtedly declined in the customer service arena, and that was a situation he was intent on rectifying. She was a natural salesperson, that was obvious. Perhaps she would consider a position in the store?

How did he know she needed work? Olivia did not ask, just as Felix did not request a resume, or inquire as to her retail experience. He simply launched right in, business-like and to the point, telling her a position had just opened—starting level, minimum wage, but commission on sales and growth potential, quarterly bonus—and inquiring as to whether Olivia was interested. "If so," he had said, "you could begin immediately. Tomorrow, even."

Olivia did not pretend to think it over. "What time would you like me to arrive?"

Now, nearly home, she can hardly believe her luck. *She has a job!* She imagines the old Olivia, with her closet of couture and her dinner parties and custom Italian furniture, being a minimum-wage retail position. How would she respond?

The current Olivia has no idea, and it doesn't matter. She isn't that person anymore. And the person she is—exhausted, disheveled, squeezed against a smudged train window—feels on top of the world.

Later that night, Olivia tells the family. Gwynnie squeals, jumping up and hugging her mother, momentarily forgetting her cool girl persona. "I knew you could do it, Mom! I was right about the hair, wasn't I?"

Gladys is less excited.

"My daughter working in retail. At your age? That's not a job for a woman like you."

"It's not like I'm swimming in options, Mom. And I think it sounds fun."

There is a pause, then Gladys smiles.

"Well, you look happy, and that's what matters. And at least it's Harper James and not some horrendous fast fashion outlet in the mall. So, darling, the most important part . . . what about a family discount?"

Chapter Seven

La'Airy, who?

For a human relations executive, Carol Ann Leyman shows a definitive lack of interpersonal skills. To put it bluntly, she's a royal bitch.

Her first day at Harper James, Olivia showed up right on time. Ten minutes early, in fact. Hair in a shiny, neat chignon, properly caffeinated and wearing a fresh coat of dusty pink lipstick—a shade that says *I'm a professional woman ready to take on the world;* she headed to the executive offices, knowing exactly where she was going. "They'll be expecting you," Felix had said. "And welcome to Harper James, Olivia."

Only Carol Ann hadn't been expecting her, or so she claimed, and welcomed was the last thing Olivia felt. A heavy-set woman in a too-tight tan polyester business suit who sported an unfortunate combination—uniboob *and* unibrow—she had glared at the new arrival, as though her very existence was an inconvenience. "Olivia who?" She had said. "And how do you know Mr. DuPaul?" Olivia had explained again and again to this bitch, the woman staring at her, unbelieving. Olivia staring right back at Carol Ann's too tight, ill-fitting blouse, flesh and black lace bra bulging in between the buttons, front and center. Olivia already felt on edge, and Carol Ann's strangeness only made the whole thing even worse.

"Wait," she finally said. "I remember. You're the one Felix called about."

Olivia had a strange suspicion she'd known the whole time.

Afterwards, there had been a barrage of questions—her retail experience? Her customer service skills? Where did she go to school? Where is she originally from? Who were her favorite designers? Why did she think she would be an asset to Harper James? iPhone or Android? Olivia had tried to remain calm, answering each with professionalism, though Carol Ann found each answer more unsatisfactory than the next. "What year was that?" Carol Ann had asked. "So, you're saying . . . you haven't worked in this industry for two decades?"

Finally, Carol Ann sighed and reached for a folder. "Well, this was Felix's call, so here's your paperwork. But just so you know, Ms. Wyatt, this is a trial run. Harper James holds employees to a high standard. And my job? To see they live up to it." Olivia quickly responds with, 'it's Kopelman. Olivia Kopelman. I've returned to my maiden name."

***

Now, finally, Olivia is to be shown her job. "Follow me," says Mrs. Leyman, then takes off down the hall in what only can be described as a Nazi march. The only missing piece was her wearing tall black boots and an armband showing her Hitler loyalty. Olivia races to catch up, knowing not to ask questions. They enter the elevator, Leyman hits the third-floor button, and they head upstairs. They stand there in stone cold silence. Olivia is grateful she didn't eat anything questionable last night or this morning. Her nausea is off the charts. *Olivia, the nausea is actually a form of anxiety,* she remembers a therapist once telling her.

Third floor! Olivia wracks her brain. *Women's contemporary*, she thinks. Not the couture level, one level up, but still high-end. The staff doors open to a long hallway, and Leyman Nazi-marches forward, uniboob bouncing, as Olivia races to keep up.

"A quick tour," Leyman says, though she does not seem to be addressing anyone, and the tour consists of her nodding her head in various directions. "Break room," she says nodding to the left. "Employee restroom," she says, nodding to the right. Olivia hardly notices, eyes focused on the doors at the end of the hall. The ones that lead to the selling floor, and her future.

Leyman pushes through, and there they are, in the warm glow of Harper James. The store will not open for an hour, so the floor is empty, except a few employees who, upon spotting Ms. Leyman, dart away, quick as rabbits.

Leyman charges ahead, barking out information about fifteen-minute breaks—*not a second more*—staff meetings and uniform maintenance. Olivia barely listens, mind spinning with possibilities. Alice + Olivia? No, they sweep right by that section. Theory? Well, it wouldn't be an advanced designer, but you gotta start somewhere . . . and yet, no. They walk right past, moving further and further into the depths of Contemporary Women's Wear.   Marc by Marc Jacobs, Joie, DKNY, Tory Burch, Diane von Furstenberg . . .

"This is it," says Leyman. "We're here."

A Wall. They've reached a *literal wall*. And pasted halfway up, in that familiar, cursive script, La'Airy!

La'Airy *is still around?* thinks Olivia. Obviously, it is still around. And she is staring right at it. Tiny and hidden in the furthest depths of the floor, against the wall, but here it is. Olivia smiles widely, trying to hide her disappointment.

"Well, Carol Ann," booms a gravelly voice. "To what do I owe the pleasure?"

A woman has appeared in front of them, and despite the force, the voice belongs to a minute figure. She stares at them, looking interested, or perhaps it is just the eyebrows, tweezed and redrawn into two sideways commas, Joan Crawford-style.

This woman is older, Olivia thinks—hell, she's elderly—yet perfectly maintained. Heavy foundation, peach blusher, nude lips with liner so sharp she might have applied it with an exacto knife. Simple pearl earrings and her hair teased, and hair sprayed to the extreme. She was a fire hazard in waiting.

A lot of work goes into being this lady, Olivia thinks. It's exhausting just looking at her! As for a specific age, that cannot be determined, though the wrinkles are obvious—no Botox or fillers or lifts for this woman. Still, the exact decade of existence does not matter. Beneath the spackled layer of war paint and painstaking efforts, Olivia can see the obvious: this woman is beautiful. With her high cheekbones, wide set brown eyes and fine bone structure, Olivia can only imagine what a knockout she must have been in her prime.

"Hello, Marguerite," says Leyman, voice even icier than usual. The super Bitch can't even pretend to try to be nice.

The two contemplate each other for a moment, the older woman taking in the HR manager's too-tight ensemble with a subtle once over—so fast, only Olivia notices—her face registering an equally quick flash of distaste. As for the woman herself—Marguerite, Olivia thinks, is wearing a familiar ensemble.

The La'Airy uniform, with its crisp white top, tweed pants, and at her neck, the striped silk scarf tied in a knot, just like a 1972 British Airlines flight attendant. Olivia recognizes it immediately despite not having seen it in years.

In her childhood, Olivia spent many hours watching her mother browse the La'Airy racks. Back then, it had been considered the height of taste for daywear amongst the moneyed set. La'Airy was the go-to for conservative pieces, and even now, glancing across the racks, Olivia sees not much has changed. Demure dresses with nipped in waists, elegant pantsuits, tea-length dresses with subtle lace accents. Everyday attire for those who summer on Nantucket—boat neck tops with quarter sleeves. And those stripes! Who could forget them? Subtle accent pieces mostly, like scarves, belts, and clutches, they scream *I can afford La'Airy* without throwing it in your face.

In recent years, they had come to signify something else: out of touch. Old-school, but not in a cool vintage way. *I mean, who wears La'Airy anymore?* Olivia is shocked they still have a department at Harper James, even one in the deepest outback recesses of the store. Truly, merchandised in the graveyard of brand placement.

"Let me introduce Olivia," says Carol Ann, without bothering to glance at her. "Your newest employee."

"I see," says Marguerite. "Felix mentioned."

"Olivia has no experience whatsoever. With intensive training, she might be of some use." Marguerite says nothing, and Olivia notes the HR woman growing visibly uncomfortable. "An extra set of hands, you know. Maybe she could help fold?" the Bitch says, voice cracking.

"I know what an assistant does, Carol Ann. I have worked here since the 1960's."

"Yes, of course, I just mean . . ."

"I'll take it from here," says Marguerite, turning towards Olivia. Carol Ann opens her mouth, thinks better of it, then turns abruptly, and exactly at 180 degrees, exits as quickly as she arrived, Nazi-marching in the other direction. Marguerite and Olivia watch the retreat in silence.

"Loathsome creature," says Marguerite. "I cannot abide a woman clad in poor fitting synthetics, and at Harper James nonetheless! It would take so little effort to secure proper underpinnings, don't you agree?" She does not wait for an answer, but continues her rapid-fire commentary, voice measured and unfailingly polite. "Fifteen minutes with Martha on the second floor lingerie department, that's all it would take. She's a wonder with the brassiere, that Martha. Especially the minimizer bra! Yet Carol Ann Leyman does not consider such things a priority." Marguerite turns to Olivia, then looks surprised, as though seeing her for the first time.

"Well, you need not worry. I see that your breasts are perfectly lifted." Olivia does not know whether to laugh or say thank you. Luckily, Marguerite does not expect an answer. "So, young lady, I was aware of your arrival. This is Felix's doing, of course."

Olivia nods.

"Olivia, was it?"

"Yes, pleasure to . . ."

"Right," says Marguerite, though she has already lost interest, spun around and is speed walking across the floor. She heads towards the back, talking as fast as she walks. Olivia races to keep up. For a senior citizen, she's fast—how old is she, even? Olivia does the calculations in her head. Started in the 60's, so she must be, hold on let me think . . ."

"I am 72," says Marguerite, as though possessing psychic abilities. "The oldest employee at Harper

James, in fact, and far past retirement. But they have made an exception, you see, as I was here in the early days. Knew Benjamin Harper myself!"

"You knew the Harpers?" says Olivia, her mind rushing with a million questions. They were legendary, the Harper family, like the retail version of the Kennedy clan. Camelot.

"Yes, yes. All dead now. Well, except the matriarch, but she's rather close to the end I've heard." She guides Olivia down a back hallway towards a nondescript doorway. "And I am soon to follow, I suppose. Oh, yes, here we are!" Marguerite turns, then bursts into laughter. "Oh, the look on your face! Now don't you worry, I have a few good years left, I'm sure."

"Well, you look amazing!"

"Indeed, and no easy task. But that is a choice, right? Life is about choices. Now, follow me."

Olivia does as she is told.

"As I am sure you are well aware, Harper James no longer requires uniforms for the salesgirls, or even interpersonal skills for that matter. The behavior can be . . . but I digress. Basic black, that is the only stipulation, with one brand serving as a refreshing exception. La'Airy is unique in that manner. Tradition, that is the La'Airy way." They enter the stockroom, and Marguerite sighs. "Well, it was."

The room is small but crammed. Racks of clothes flank the walls, only they are unlike any La'Airy garments Olivia has ever seen. Billowy blouses and poofy skirts, silhouettes far from La'Airy's iconic and tailored refinement, and if that were not bad enough, the stripes are a far cry from the subtlety of yore. Horizontal slashes, thick enough to make a size 2 look frumpy, and some even . . . oh God . . . glittered as the bedazzled Las Vegas strip.

Olivia's eyes hurt.

There are other pieces too, vaguely familiar, only somehow skewed. The French cuffs, only now edged in pink sequins. The classic cocktail dresses, just with an overdose of tulle and slut-worthy plunging necklines.

"I know what you must be thinking," says Marguerite, observing with pinched lips. "Hideous." Marguerite gives a sardonic laugh. "The fall collection. A new direction for the company, or so I've been informed by corporate." The old woman sighs. "Between you and me, the shipment arrived a week ago, but I just can't bear to bring it out to the floor. It's incredibly hideous!"

A sigh, wave of the hand, and Marguerite jumps back into action, striding towards a jumbled tower at the back of the stockroom—disregarded hangers, a broken full-length mirror, stacked boxes. Behind the mess there is the sound of clanking and rattling. Merchandisers looking for something. "Excuse the mayhem!" she says through the clamor. You see, it has only been me for several years, and I tend to neglect this area. No excuse, really, as I have plenty of time on my hands. In fact, that is exactly what I told Felix. 'Why would I need an associate?' There is Elise the part-timer to fill in during an absence, and those are rare. Can count the number of days I have missed over the course of decades. That said, I do welcome your company." More clanging, and Olivia watches the boxes rattle, her head doing the same. "Sweet Felix, he still holds out hope, poor boy . . . believes you might be of some help, but I tend towards the realistic . . . oh yes! Here we go!"

She emerges, triumphant, holding a pair of tweed pants, white blouse sans sequins, and striped scarf.

"Just your size, too," says Marguerite. "A 6, correct?" Olivia nods. "Trust me. I've been at this since you were an embryo."

Marguerite leaves her to change in the stock room, and Olivia tries to focus, pushing away all her gnawing concerns as she pulls on the tweed pants and aligns the tips of her French cuffs. She was right; the uniform is a perfect fit. Olivia stares at herself in a full-length mirror, remembering this is what she wanted. A new start.

But . . . La'Airy?

Okay, so she had hoped for another brand, some-thing glamorous, but this was just a launching pad. Who cares that the department is hidden away, like a dirty little secret, or that the tacky and dated sequined get up is her new work uniform? She loves fashion; once she had hoped this industry would be her life. Now, all these years later, she has an opportunity few will ever get.

A second chance.

Olivia will succeed. She will make money, move out of her childhood bedroom. She will sell, charm cus-tomers, rise in the ranks. Okay, so she's older than most employees, but Felix saw something in her, and she will prove him right. And this is truly a fresh start—Felix knows her background, but he's sworn not to utter a word to anyone. Olivia believes him.

This is the new me, she thinks, staring into the mirror against the wall, face hard with determination. A quick dusting of powder and blusher—a nod to her supervi-sor's extensive cosmetic efforts—and Olivia deems her-self ready. Only . . . the lipstick? That deep pink shade that made her feel so powerful that morning is not this department's aesthetic, exactly. She should wipe it off and opt for a more subtle tint; English Rose, Apricot Sunset or Spring ranunculus might be better.

No, thinks Olivia, impulsively digging the tube from her bag and adding another layer. Swipe, rub, smack and . . . there. She feels suddenly powerful, protected by her pink armor.

Olivia is ready, and once she emerges on the floor, Marguerite seems to agree. She gives an approving nod, then circles her, adjusting the uniform. "Very good," she confirms. "Now the pièce de la résistance." Marguerite goes behind the counter and emerges, a striped scarf dangling from her hand. "The La'Airy bow. Come."

The two stand in front of the trifold mirror. "Just follow along, my Dear," she says, modeling on her own neck. "Cross over the pieces, longer at bottom, yes, now cinch, loop—keep it taut, now—pull and . . . secure! Look at that. On your very first try!"

Olivia smiles at the woman's reflection.

"Welcome," says Marguerite. "To La'Airy!"

For the rest of the morning, Olivia is shown the tiny department in detail, Marguerite introducing her to each piece and offering commentary. She is versed in ringing up purchases on the computer, tagging inventory and shown the La'Airy way to display accessories. The woman never stops talking, and it occurs to Olivia how happy she seems to finally have company. La'Airy, Olivia soon realizes, could be a lonely place.

But not one customer. Unless you count that woman looking for the restrooms.

At 12:15, Marguerite announces Olivia's lunch break. "Forty-five minutes, and not a minute longer. You'll be going out, I take it?"

"I brought my lunch."

"Oh," says Marguerite, a flash of concern crossing her face. "Well, I suppose the break room, then."

"I saw it on the tour," says Olivia. "But what about you? When will you take lunch?"

"Oh sweetheart," says Marguerite. "I stopped eating in 1982." She laughs. "One day you'll understand. After sixty, it goes to hell and hell. Forget any handbasket."

Olivia gives her a skeptical look. "You're tiny!"

"My point exactly. No lunch. But you should eat, so go."

Marguerite goes back to adjusting the racks of clothing for nonexistent customers. "Oh, and Olivia?"

Olivia turns.

"Beware of wolves in Chanel suits."

***

Unnerved by Marguerite's warning, Olivia contemplates forgoing the break room for one of those 5th Avenue bodega buffets, or even a Starbucks. In the end, she nixes the idea, refusing to pay for overpriced coffee or congealed macaroni salad. Besides, she is officially a Harper James girl now, a member of the community, the family.

Olivia will go to the break room, just like any other Harper James employee. Why is she worrying? She's fun, right? A firecracker, that's what everyone used to say. *Olivia is an absolute riot.*

Renewed by her own self-Dr. Phil-like pep talk, Olivia lifts her chin and strides towards the back hallway. *You got this,* she thinks. What does Oprah say? *Live your truth, Olivia. Own it. Be your best . . . oh, whatever.*

Fuck that, she thinks. *Just be a normal person. A normal person having lunch.*

***

Never take Oprah-isms in vain, that's the lesson.

Thirty-two minutes later, Olivia sits in a corner of the break room feeling both invisible and utterly on display.

Forget being your best you. All Olivia has succeeded in is being the freak nibbling egg salad in the corner and pretending she doesn't care that no one will talk to her.

They've noticed her, though. That's for sure. Olivia couldn't blend in if she tried.

For starters, there's the uniform. Tradition may be innate to La'Airy, but in the Harper James break room, it just makes you look like some weird throwback. Vintage, but not the cool kind you get in a boutique—more like some old lady castoffs you score at a Hadassah swap meet. Or a *WTC* charity event.

In the La'Airy department, the uniform looks right. But here she is totally aware of her outsider status. There's the fact that the other sales associates wear black, of course, but that's just part of it. Harper James has a reputation, and you can see it on every associate. These aren't the basic check-out girls at Forever 21, that's for sure. However, they do seem to put in a lot of effort. Never mind the color limitation, these girls have style, and they dress the part.

Girls flutter in and out of the room, grabbing diet drinks from the soda machine. They travel in duos, or gather in clusters, and Olivia knows who they are without exchanging a word. She doesn't have much choice there, and alone in the corner, there's plenty of time to observe.

There are the girls specializing in boho couture, à la Rachel Zoe, with their beachy hair, long skirts and peasant-inspired tops; the former sorority girls and debs who sell to customers as pretty as they are, looking Hamptons ready in their flirty little dresses. Those from the

Young Contemporary department, unapologetic in their patterned tights and strategic cut-outs, who act to the age group they sell. They are the loudest and most annoying. Gathered at a table across the room, they're laughing too loud, taking selfies and side-eyeing everyone who crosses their path. Periodically, they glance at Olivia and lean in to whisper among themselves. Obviously gossiping about her. They aren't the only ones.

Not that anyone has bothered to introduce themselves. Smiles have been returned by careless and diverted eyes. It's like a middle school lunchroom, and Olivia's the weird new kid from another country, or a cult maybe—the kind where they force you to wear tweed pants, pink sequined edged French cuffs and a striped bow around your neck. Olivia thinks, *this damn bow feels more like a noose than any fashion accessory.*

Olivia is the oldest one here by a decade. The place is practically oozing every younger generation. Generation Z and Millennials. She knows what they are all thinking: *why the hell did they hire her? She's, like, old. I mean, in her forties! Bet it was a favor. Bet she knows someone in management, no, she's fucking someone. Maybe she was desperate, needed help. Fell on hard times, or some other totally depressing story . . .*

They wouldn't be wrong.

Olivia tells herself to stop. No one cares, she thinks. Why are you so insecure? In D.C., she could work any room, even one full of the most uptight rich bitches. So why is she intimidated by a bunch of . . . Harper James amateur employees?

Olivia checks her watch. 13 minutes to go. That'll give her five minutes to get back to La'Airy. She will stick it out, she's determined. After all, she made it this far. Who cares what they think, *arrogant mother fuckers!*

Olivia has spent the entire lunch pretending just that. Sitting in an uncomfortable metal chair, back against the cement block wall, pretending not to care. Pretending she is perfectly happy to scroll through her phone and eat her sandwich. Really, there is no cell signal, so she just scrolls through old text messages. And as for the sandwich, it came in a brown paper bag with her name scrawled across the front in bright red Sharpie.

Talk about middle school.

Gladys had insisted, looking so hopeful when she handed off the bag that morning. While not a fan of her daughter working retail, Olivia could tell her mother was happy to see her doing something other than sprawl across the couch and watch trashy daytime TV. "I made your lunch," she had said, oozing hope from every pore. Back then, only a few hours ago, Olivia had felt the

155

same thing. She'd even taken the bag with a smile despite the fact she was way too old for an egg salad sandwich wrapped in plastic wrap and a Ziploc with three Oreos. Even a lemonade juice box. The part she couldn't believe was the note Gladys enclosed: "Wash your hands (lots of Corona germs out there!), be careful crossing the street, don't talk to strangers!"

Now she's grateful. Since there's no one to talk to, eating at least gives her something to do.

Then, the voice of someone.

"Are you new?"

The voice is soft, almost whispery. Olivia looks up eagerly; a girl stares down at her, blue eyes wide with curiosity.

"Hi!" says Olivia, sounding way too eager. "Yes, just started. I'm Olivia."

The girl doesn't offer her name or even respond. She cocks her head to the side and continues to gaze at Olivia, like observing some almost extinct species of animal in the zoo.

Olivia cannot help but do the same. Just like her, this girl stands out.

She can't be much over twenty-two, and beautiful in that effortless way. She's small, maybe 5'2", with delicate bones, pore-less skin and the kind of white-blonde hair favored by classic movie stars and surfer chicks.

The kind of hair that rarely works in real life, except on her, it seems just right.

She wears a simple white sheath dress that falls just above her perfectly golden knees—*tanning bed? Spray tan? Weekend in Ibiza?* Olivia cannot pinpoint the brand she's wearing. Expensive, that's obvious, and probably Italian. Not the kind of thing a young sales girl wears, that's for damn sure. In the sea of black, she is like an exotic orchid, the human version of a *fuck you* to everyone else in the room.

Who is this chick? And why is she staring at Olivia, eyes wide open and curious, but not saying a damn word? The seconds tick by, Olivia scrambling for something to say, the girl passively observing her discomfort as though it's a party trick.

One bright pop of color—a silky, carnation-yellow scarf. It has been breezily looped, like a total afterthought and final touch, like you'd see in some European film. *Shall we go on a jaunt? Board the yacht? Yes, yes, just let me throw on my carnation-yellow scarf and grab the chardonnay! Wow, my scarf and the wine are the same color! Omg, no way!*

Suddenly, Olivia's La'Airy bow feels even tighter. It just may choke her.

Olivia has had enough. "So, yes I just . . ."

"You don't really work at La'Airy, do you?"

157

The words are just as quiet as before; she needs to lean in to hear. At the same time, they waft through the air like a terrible odor.

Olivia nods.

"Oh, I see," says the girl. Then she laughs. Unlike her speech, the giggle is high-pitched and shrill, filling the room. Olivia glances around to see if anyone is watching. Of course, they are. In fact, she's pretty sure the half-dozen women have been watching for quite a while, and no one is bothering to be subtle. A girl at the soda machine stares, mouth hanging open and quarter frozen halfway in the slot. Another holds a dangling tea bag over a steaming mug. Even the young Contemporary girls have looked up from their phones, ceasing to insta-sext to carefully observe the scene.

The girl stops laughing suddenly. "That's hilarious," she says matter-of-factly. "They actually hired someone. It's like that last gasp, right? Before you totally die."

"What do you mean?"

She leans in. "Oh," she says, her whisper now meant only for Olivia. "You thought it was a real job? That's so sad." The girl takes a step back, eyes brimming with sympathy. Faux-sympathy, sure, but the only emotion she has shown beyond mocking curiosity and laughter. "They should have told you! La'Airy is like totally over. Finito. I hear they won't make it through the winter selling season. Fourth quarter. But between you and me, it's . . . it's totally time. I mean, c'mon, you gotta admit . . . who wears stuff like that anymore? Besides old ladies."

Olivia feels the anger rise. Who is this obnoxious person? Fuck her and her pore-less skin. Olivia hasn't done a thing to this girl, so why is she the target of this middle school, mean girl BS? And who is she to judge anyway? She can't be corporate . . . she wasn't in black, and they don't do break rooms. Just some little girl in a white dress—okay, the dress is pretty great, Olivia will give her that, waltzing around with her whispered judgments. What the hell does she know about La'Airy?

Amateur.

Sitting alone, being ignored, the judgment . . . in that moment, Olivia feels every injustice rumbling up from inside her. For six months, she has been nothing but raw nerves. There has been shock, confusion, and tears. Suddenly, she feels a rush of confidence. "That's one opinion," says Olivia, sharp and cold as an icicle. "La'Airy is classic, iconic. Those versed in fashion history understand the nuances, but really, it isn't your fault." Olivia smiles at the girl. "You're young. You have plenty of time to learn about artistry and craftsmanship."

159

Shout-out to Marguerite, thinks Olivia, drunk on her own recklessness. *That's what happens when you play with the big girls.*

That's when she remembers: they have an audience. Olivia glances around, noting the looks of horror, the wide eyes. No one will meet her gaze.

Olivia does not give a shit.

Most horrified of all? The girl in the white dress. For a split-second, Olivia sees the fury across her face. A clench of the jaw, a flare of the nostril, fury beaming like red lasers from those horror movie doll eyes.

Just as quickly, it is over. Her face melts right back into pretty neutrality, like nothing ever happened. She even smiles.

"Well, Olivia," she says lightly. "Welcome to the Harper James family!"

A little giggle, a turn, and she flits towards the break room door. Just like that, she's gone.

It's like nothing happened. Right away, the room goes back to the pre-millennial run-in scene. Teabags are dunked, quarters dropped in slots. There is chatter again, gossip between the Contemporary girls.

Olivia turns to a woman at the nearest table, only a few feet away. She's the only one sitting alone. "Hey," says Olivia, but the woman pretends not to hear. Olivia repeats herself, and the woman turns, looking completely annoyed. She is dressed in sharp lines and hard edges, *a German designer, Jil Sander possibly . . .* Olivia figures—and she's obviously got the personality to match.

"What?" she hisses.

"You know that girl? In the white dress?"

Edgy rolls her eyes. "Of course. Everyone knows the Salon Girls."

"What's a Salon Girl?"

The girl snorts. "Personal Shopping department," she says, as though Olivia was mentally challenged.

Of course! Olivia had forgotten that place existed, but she knew exactly what it was. The Salon was a legend, in fact.

"Look, it doesn't matter anyway. You'll hardly ever see any of them. The Salon Girls barely ever leave the 5th Floor."

"But that girl . . .?"

"Yeah, I mean, they show up now and then." The girl looks away, obviously done with the conversation. "Most people know to leave them alone."

Leave them alone? Why? The place has a reputation, but they're not exactly celebrities or the Harper James CEO.

Before Olivia can ask how many personal shoppers there are, or what their credentials might be, or why that girl was such a complete bitch, she notices the clock.

Oh shit. She jumps to her feet, practically racing to the door.

My first day, thinks Olivia. *Off to a great fucking start.*

***

Back at La'Airy, Marguerite is staring at her watch as Olivia arrives. "Ten minutes late," she says looking up. "At La'Airy, promptness is . . ."

One look at Olivia's face, and Marguerite sighs and shakes her head. "Wolves in Chanel, I tell you. I was afraid of this. Cold shoulders, I take it? I suspected as much. No etiquette, this tech generation. In my early years, we girls knew the value of good social graces."

"Is La'Airy in trouble?" Olivia can't help it. The words just shoot out of her mouth.

Marguerite glances around, as if there were actual customers in earshot. She takes Olivia's elbow and guides her towards the back, where they are hidden behind the on-sale 75% off cashmere sweater sets.

"So, is it? Is La'Airy in trouble?"

"I thought you knew that my dear. That's why you're here. A last-ditch effort to up sales. A pointless endeavor, but that is Felix's way. Always hopeful, the lovely man, even when the writing's on the wall." Eyes misty, Marguerite forces a smile. "La'Airy is a sinking ship, Olivia. But don't worry yourself. We will have a grand time, the two of us. It's much more fun to sink with company around!"

The flash of an image crosses Olivia's mind. A white dress, red laser doll-eyes, a pretty, smug stare. *That last gasp, right? Before you totally die.*

"I suppose there's only one option," says Olivia, matter-of-factly.

"Exactly," says Marguerite. "We need to sell."

Chapter Eight

The Truly Dire Nature of the Situation

"Deceased. Cancer," Marguerite whispers and then clicks her tongue, moving to the next card. "Oh yes, her as well . . . stroke, I believe. Or was it Alzheimer's? Oy."

Marguerite clicks her tongue again and flips through the cards. And sighs.

Olivia sighs too, watching Marguerite go through her ancient rolodex—yes, the kind that nobody has used in decades, with a handle to spin the contraption, while chirpily delivering the unfortunate news with each slightly yellowed and tattered card.

"Gone, gone. Lovely funeral, though. The flower arrangements were divine. White lilies and roses in Czech crystal vases. Married into Standard Oil money."

"There must be someone," interrupts Olivia, trying to keep her voice light, positive. Who is she doing it for? Pointless, this whole endeavor, but Olivia has already run out of ideas, *first day jitters,* she thinks.

"Oh!" says Marguerite. "Here's one!" Olivia raises her eyebrows, hopeful.

"Still kicking, I believe. Just let me think for a moment," says Marguerite, closing her eyes. "She got married again, that's right. To her sister's husband. Très scandalous. Of course, the sister was long gone, but still. Who wanted to miss that wedding? Billionaires, both of them. Lovely home on the UES, a classic six. I rarely made home visits, but for her . . . yes, I am sure she is at the same address! I'll try this number, you never know." Marguerite lifts the receiver of their 20th century landline phone and starts dialing. Olivia hopes the phone even works because it looks so old.

Marguerite drops it into the cradle just as fast.

"Yes. St. Lucia, of course. That's where they retired. It's coming back to me now."

Olivia fights the urge to roll her eyes, instead forcing an understanding smile.

"Before she passed, that is. Blood clot."

"I'm sorry, my dear. It has been eons since the days of my regular clients."

"It's been a long time, of course!" says Olivia. "I'm amazed you remember so much. There must be someone though. If you think hard, I mean, maybe someone will come to mind."

Marguerite returns her smile with a sad one. "I applaud your initiative, my dear. But you see, this is a rather futile exercise."

"There must be someone."

"These aren't *someone's*," snaps Marguerite. "Back in the day, my clients were the pinnacle of society. Married to titans yet forces of nature in their own right. And the style! No matter the occasion, be it purchasing groceries or lunching at the La's—Grenouille and Caravelle, I mean—they would rather die than be caught sans stockings, lipstick, and gloves. The Gloria Guinness's, the CZ Guest's, even the Jackie O's. And when in search of the perfect cocktail sheath, or the ideal capri pants for those summer afternoons on the Vineyard, well whom did they seek out?"

Marguerite has gone somewhere else—to another time. Olivia reaches out, gently resting her hand on Marguerite's frail one.

"You," says Olivia. "Of course, they came to you."

"Indeed," says Marguerite. A tiny sigh, and she pulls her hand away. "But those days are gone, and we must live in the present." She lifts the rolodex and heads for the stockroom, Olivia on her tail.

"You can't think of anyone, Marguerite?"

"Well, the dead ones at least. I am sorry, my dear." Marguerite turns to Olivia, assessing her from across the newly organized stockroom. "As I said, I appreciate your get up and go. The fighter spirit will serve you well. But La'Airy's survival, I am afraid, is a battle even you will not win. Besides, what good will it do? Even if I could drum up a client—in a manner that did not require exhuming a body, excuse my obscenity—what good would it do anyway? You made the acquaintance of Miss Ginger Johnson, or have you forgotten?" Olivia nods. "And you will meet her again, I am sure of that. She is the only regular we have."

***

One week into her new position, Olivia has come to understand the truly dire nature of the situation.

Five days, three sales. Approximately forty hours . . . and . . . a . . . miserable . . . three . . . sales.

Number one had been to an older woman, mid-sixties, who was effortlessly dressed. She had appeared like an apparition on Olivia's second day, planting herself in the center of the La'Airy department. "I need assistance!" She barked at no one in particular. "Does anyone work here?"

She was looking straight at Olivia as she said it.

"You take this client," Marguerite had whispered. "Don't worry, Olivia. You're ready."

At first, Olivia had been excited, doting on the woman as she pointed out numerous items. "The cream double-breasted blazer? Casual, yet elegant. And the color will look marvelous against your . . ."

"Yes," the woman interrupted. "I want that. And the black satin tuxedo pants and bracelet sleeved, knee-length navy dress too. I have a few events coming up that they would be perfect for." Olivia delivered item after item to the dressing room, hardly believing her luck. Only two days into the job and look at her! She would single handedly save La'Airy . . . just wait and see. As for the woman, while never warm, she had been welcoming to Olivia's help, asking for a thorough critique of each ensemble. This took a while, as each change took an annoying minimum of twenty minutes, but Olivia was more than happy to help. Her first client!

Hours later, Olivia had rung up purchase after purchase, euphoria rising with the sales numbers. This was going to be huge! She thought *oh my god, check out all these zero's! I will make my monthly sales goal! (*During her interview with Miss Adolf, she was told that, "You will have strict and fierce monthly sales goals to meet. But please know that your obvious lack of industry experience will not be an excuse for low sales numbers.") Across the department, Marguerite watched from the corner of her eye, strangely moved. The time came for the credit card, and just as Olivia reached for it, fingers already tingling in plastic anticipation, the woman stepped back, credit card still in hand.

"You know, thinking this through . . ."

The belt. That's all she wanted. Simple and black with a horseshoe buckle, it was a low-end item. Even more, from the tiny sales section, a mere fourth of the original tag price.

$69.50.

It took all her strength to stay calm as Olivia wrapped up the purchase and bid the woman goodbye. Once they were alone again, Marguerite magically appeared, patting Olivia on the shoulder. "Ginger. She does that once a week."

"Why didn't you tell me?"

"You needed the practice," said Marguerite. Her expression was serious, though Olivia could make out the faintest hint of a smile. "Excellent, my dear. Now, let us look at your work on the pantsuit rack . . . as I mentioned before, the hangers should be of equal distance apart. 2.5 inches from one to another."

Sale number two had been an exasperated teenage girl seeking a gift for her grandmother. "I guess this will work," she had said, grabbing the first thing she spotted—a floral printed scarf right by the counter. "Grammy is, like, super old," she said, holding the scarf as though it were on fire. "She loves this stuff."

Sale 2: $39.95. Another on sale item.

Finally, a frazzled and middle-aged woman had shown up, announced she was late for a meeting, freezing her ass off and had forgotten a sweater. "Just anything neutral," she had said, then reached for a black cropped jacket on the sale rack and threw it on the counter. "Here, this will work . . . I don't need a bag . . . oh, wait a second, what's your return policy?" she asked as she slipped the jacket over the black sweater set, she was already wearing.

Sale 3: $119.49.

Barely over a hundred bucks! Olivia felt deflated. She had done everything she could think of to drum up business, despite her limited client book. She had scouted other departments, trailing shoppers, and suggesting they might check out La'Airy's newest delivery. At best, they had given her a dismissive smile. More often, they simply looked confused, or said something like, *La'Airy? That brand is still around? Wow. Interesting.*

There, hidden in the depths of the second-floor recesses, Olivia felt invisible. Since her unfortunate encounter in the break room, she stayed to herself and always chose to exit Harper James entirely during free moments—at lunch, she would eat on a park bench, or grab a piece of pizza from any random place close by.

In the luxury world of Harper James, La'Airy was the forgotten fat and ugly stepchild. The only times Olivia ran into other sales associates were in the elevator or on trips to the restroom. Even then, she felt like a pariah, as though others were going to great lengths to avoid her. Smiles were not returned, and eye contact was always quickly broken.

Word travels fast at Harper James, come to find out, and personnel conflicts are frowned upon. At least, that was the case when the conflict involved a Salon Girl.

Harper James was like a foreign country, Olivia had come to understand, whose individual brand cultures, rules, and etiquette she could not fathom. Only one thing was clear—in this kingdom, there was a distinct hierarchy, and Salon Girls were at the very top.

"They barely ever leave the 5th Floor," the girl in the break room had said. "You'll never see them." Unless they want you to, Olivia had come to discover. Then you could not miss them, even if you tried.

The first Salon Girl sighting had come on Wednesday, and Olivia heard them before she saw them.

Olivia had been straightening a rack of cardigans when giggling cut through the air. She had looked up, only to see two girls turn the corner, looking like a mirage in warm Harper James lighting. Both were average height, maybe 5'5", and wearing flirty cocktail dresses.

They did not appear to be shoppers, nor did they seem to be in any particular rush—though one looked ready for sorority rush. Pastel peach dress, diamond ear studs, Cartier gold love bracelets and, despite the January icy forecast, bare feet in Chanel ballet flats. The other was her exact opposite in a skin-tight black dress and towering heels—she looked more club-ready than mid-day retail establishment. Yet, despite the opposing looks, they looked disconcertingly similar, like they could be twins. Bright blond hair and pretty faces—not exceptionally pretty, but the everyday kind—and their most arresting feature of all. The boobs.

They weren't really that large—maybe C-cups—but they stood out. High up, too. For the sorority-looking one, her boobs seemed to defy gravity, lifted so high, Olivia wondered if she would actually lift off the floor. The other had gone the more obvious route, plunging into the dangerously low cut zone.

Either way, their chests drew attention, as they were meant to—it was as if they arrived first, the girls following closely behind the boob finish line.

Olivia told herself not to stare, glancing towards the rack she was working on—*good*, she had thought. *They didn't notice . . . they don't even know I'm here.* Yet, as they walked by, both stopped mid-giggle, eyes sliding simultaneously towards . . .

Olivia.

It was bizarre, giving Olivia the chills. She felt like she had been spotted by those twins in *The Shining,* only the inflated breast versions.

***

Thursday, it happened again. Same weirdness, different Salon Girl. This time, Olivia was behind the counter with Marguerite. A woman came storming down the aisle in heavy platform boots and a wide-shouldered jacket, slashes of metallic eyeshadow shimmering. Just like before, she had slowed down while passing La'Airy, then turned her face suddenly, gazing directly at Olivia.

A quick up and down, pinch of the lips, eye flash, and it was over.

Marguerite had clicked her tongue.

Olivia knew not to inquire further. She had made enemies, that was obvious. Watching her sink right along with La'Airy? That was a show the Salon Girls did not want to miss. Again, that high-pitched giggle had echoed through her head, as it had every day of her first week. Then she heard that smug voice from the break room in her head, each word like hot needles puncturing her eyes.

Oh, you thought it was a real Harper James job? La'Airy is totally over!

Olivia had faced public disgrace on a national level, and she was not about to do it again. "Hey," she had said, turning to Marguerite. "Do you keep any client records?"

***

Turns out, Marguerite did have records. Only to find out, they were relics of a bygone era, full of ghosts and ancient legacies. Still in old-school files, covered with decades of dust, and full of landline telephone numbers and memories of the great La'Airy days.

Still, Olivia wasn't about to quit.

"There must be a way to drum up business," she concluded, forcing a confident smile. "What was it you said when I tried on my uniform? Fashion fades, only style remains the same. You said it yourself, Marguerite."

"Actually, it was Coco Chanel who said it. And I do not believe she was speaking of La'Airy."

They needed to resurrect the fledgling brand from the fashion wastelands, reminding customers of more glamorous times. *What we need is a promotion,* thinks Olivia. *Something fabulous, enticing.* They needed an event, and Olivia knows how to plan one, that is for sure. All those years in the *WTC,* orchestrating silent auctions and disease-of-the-month fundraisers, planning center-pieces, and seating charts, hiring bands and caterers . . . and last-minute dinner parties. That had to be good for something, right?

There was only one difference: a budget. Or in this case, no budget.

"What about a mixer? A trunk show, that kind of thing. I mean, La'Airy is trying to reinvent itself, right? They must have a budget."

Marguerite snorts.

"Who is in charge of that stuff?"

"The corporate office. But I highly doubt . . ."

"What do we have to lose?" blurts Olivia, voice louder than intended. Marguerite stares at her, unreadable. "Sorry, I just . . . look, there's no harm in asking, right?"

"Debatable," says Marguerite, then sighs. "Oh, why not? If anything, your timing is ideal."

"It is?"

Marguerite taps her watch. "Friday, near closing. In twenty or so minutes, our weekly appointment will arrive. I did not mention this before so as to not overwhelm you. I believe in keeping up troop morale, especially in the face of a seemingly unwinnable battle." Marguerite laughs. "Or, in this case, a real bitch."

Chapter Nine

Anger. Concern. Fear.

Olivia cannot help but be excited. It feels like fate, or timing, or just dumb luck. In less than a half hour, she will be introduced to Lauren Lugo, from the La'Airy corporate office.

"She's new to the company," Marguerite explains. "Brought in to help, how shall we say? Revamp the brand. Apparently, she is a well-known image consultant. Whatever that means."

Beyond that information, Marguerite offers no further elaboration, other than the fact the meeting will be brief. She eyes the aisle, waiting.

There is no chance of missing Lauren; when she finally arrives, she makes her presence known. Olivia hears her before seeing her.

"Are you kidding?" barks a voice. "No way that meeting can be postponed!" Seconds later, the speaker appears, speed-walking her way down the second-floor aisle towards La'Airy.

Mid-twenties, at the very most, Lauren's wardrobe is tastefully understated, her blazer and flared pants tailored to a personally trained and toned body. What really stands out are her tech accessories: iPad under one arm, cell phones in both hands and a futuristic lighted headset in which she barks orders. "Tuesday with the mock-ups," she says, striding into the department. She heads straight for the counter where Marguerite, despite the loud interruptions, does not look up. "I've told them, this is a deadline. For a top firm, this lag time is completely . . ."

Olivia is in her line of vision and has stepped forward, wearing her most winning smile. *Introduce yourself*, she thinks. *Make a good impression.*

". . . unacceptable!" says Lauren, sweeping right by.

Once she has reached the back of the store, the call abruptly ends, and Lauren stands there, staring at Marguerite, who does not look up from the computer.

"Marguerite," she says. Marguerite does not answer right away. After a long pause, she slowly lifts her head.

"Lauren," she says, without a flicker of emotion on her face.

"We need to make this quick. I have a meeting at corporate in 45."

"Indeed," says Marguerite. Another pause.

"Let's see the numbers, then," says Lauren, storming around the counter to join her. "Go ahead, pull them up."

Marguerite does as she's told, her pace achingly slow.

"Hmm. Just a moment, please," she tells Lauren. You know these computer systems . . . they can be so slow."

Not even half a minute, but enough for Lauren to contemplate the state of her French manicure, bounce on her heels, run both hands through her glossy black hair, check the time on both phones, roll her eyes and sigh.

"Are we almost there? I don't have all day!"

"Almost!" sings Marguerite, annoyed.

Lauren scans the floor, eyes passing over Olivia as though she were a mannequin or a piece of furniture.

"Soon?"

"Mmmm-hmmmm," says Marguerite.

Lauren continues to scope out the floor. Suddenly, a revelation, her face transforming. It is less than a few seconds, but Olivia catches the flash of changing emotion. The instantaneous dropping of a harried, highly controlled façade.

Anger. Concern. Fear.

Lauren catches herself, expression returning to normal. She has no idea Olivia is there, watching from behind the cardigans.

"Marguerite," says Lauren, voice monotone. "Where is the new delivery?"

"In the stock room, of course." She is still at work on the computer.

"I thought we talked about this, Marguerite. It should have been out a week ago."

"Oh yes, that's right. Terribly sorry. Must have slipped my mind!"

"The fall collection *slipped your mind*?"

Olivia moves closer, adjusting merchandise. She doesn't want to miss a word.

"I apologize. You see, I'm terribly old. At my age, details tend to get lost in the shuffle. Especially those unworthy of my attention in the first place."

Lauren is momentarily at a loss for words. "Your job is not to critique the collections. Your job is to sell them."

"Yes, yes," says Marguerite, with a wave of her hand. "We'll put the collection out tonight, Olivia and I, assuredly. You've met Olivia, yes?" She motions towards the floor. "That's her, hidden behind the cardigans."

Lauren glances over. Seeing her chance, Olivia steps forward with a beaming smile. Lovely to meet you, Ms. Lugo," says Olivia. "I'm so excited to . . ."

Lauren has already turned her back to Marguerite. "What? A new hire? Who approved this?"

"I haven't the foggiest," says Marguerite. "Upper management, perhaps? I do not keep abreast of these things. My job is to—*how did you put it?* —sell. But please do not fret, we'll put out the new collection this very evening." Marguerite smiles warmly. "But if we were to be honest, dear," she says, voice low, "It won't make a lick of difference either way. The writing is on the wall, is it not? Or in the monthly sales reports, in this case."

Marguerite steps back, motioning to the screen as would a magician before his grand reveal. Lauren focuses on the data in front of her. Both eyes and mouth wide open with shock.

***

A few minutes later, the meeting comes to a merciful end. Lauren once again scans the figures, grunting in frustration at the weak sales numbers. Some under her breath muttering, types a few notes in one iPhone, and she steps back with a sigh.

"Abysmal," she says. "Just . . . get them up, okay?"

"Okay," says Marguerite. Lauren shakes her head. They stare at each other for a second, and Olivia realizes they have performed this routine many times before.

"Okay, gotta go," says Lauren. Instantly, she rushes to retrieve her various tech devices, ready to high-tail it out of the third-floor morgue-hellhole and get on with her life. Third-floor rear placement was the death of any brand if it hadn't already died. Everything worthy was immediately visible directly off the elevator. The second floor was always considered prime real estate for placement of the most luxurious brands.

Marguerite does not respond. Instead, she gazes across the floor warily. One meeting, and the shrewd, opinionated older woman has transformed, the life seeming to have drained from her very body. She stares off into space, eyes distant, face wan. For all the effort she takes with her appearance, her immaculate makeup and carefully constructed hair, in that moment she looks void of life. She looks exactly how she described herself: old.

Finally, Olivia understands. This weekly visit, this Lauren-and-Marguerite-show, is not meant to offer help, insight, or analysis—it is a perfunctory engagement. A means by which to chronicle the inevitable beginning of an end.

Lauren isn't there to improve business, rather she has been brought in to access and make the tough choices. To shut down the La'Airy Harper James division. That decision was made long ago, and both she and Marguerite know it. The time has come.

And Marguerite? After decades of loyalty and a wholehearted belief that classic sophistication lies in the ideal sweater set and teal-length skirt is no longer willing to fight.

Olivia, on the other hand, does not give up so easily. She also has nothing to lose.

Her items collected; Lauren Lugo gives a cursory goodbye. Before Olivia has a chance to stop her, she walks right past her. Olivia glances at Marguerite, who raises her eyebrows, as if to say, *what did you expect?*

Olivia is no quitter. She half jogs towards the aisle, catching Lauren just as she turns in the direction of the elevators.

"Excuse me? Ms. Lugo?"

Lauren freezes mid-stomp. She turns around, bristling with annoyance. The ten minutes till closing bells and announcements have already come, and final purchases hurried towards exhausted salespeople. There is no one else in the vicinity—just Lauren Lugo staring at Olivia as though she were the last unsold pathetic items on last season's sale rack.

"Yes?" says Lauren.

And Marguerite. Though she cannot know for sure, Olivia senses the older woman watching them from the La'Airy floor, and pictures her looking the same way she did when Lauren ran through the sales numbers— her face wary, her eyes distant.

"Yes?" says Lauren, glancing at her watch. "Can I help you?"

"I know sales have been slow," says Olivia.

Lauren snorts. "Um, yes, you could say that. Quite unimpressive."

"But I have a different perspective, as a new hire. You know, I just love the brand. What a legacy! And I think, if we were given the resources, we might be able to get sales numbers up."

Lauren raises her eyebrows.

"Oh yeah?"

"I was thinking . . . well, Marguerite and I were discussing the issue at length, and . . . I had an idea."

"Oh, really? An idea?" says Lauren, looking bored. "Do tell me about this *idea* you have."

"A promotional event. Nothing elaborate necessarily, you know, just a closed gathering for, well, loyal customers."

Now Lauren is interested, but not in the way one would hope. Interested like those passing the scene of a car wreck or watching a stranger's grocery bag bust open on the street. "I see. And who, exactly, would put this together?"

"We would. I have quite a bit of experience in the fundraising world, and . . ."

"Look, Olivia, was it? Olivia . . . I'm late."

"I know, just one more minute . . ."

Lauren rolls her neck in a circle. Crack.

"What exactly are you asking me for, Olivia?" Her tone is flat, dismissive.

"A budget. Corporate must have some funding for these kinds of events. Nothing enormous, just enough to organize a small event."

Lauren simply laughs. "That is not a possibility," she says.

Olivia is suddenly upset. Who is this woman? She comes from money, Olivia can tell. The bearing and sense of entitlement. But who is she, really? Some twenty-something with a marketing degree and good connections. Some random girl who makes $150k a year to waltz in and shit all over an elderly woman's decades of loyalty?

Olivia spent years around older versions of Lauren. Once, her type flocked to Olivia.

They invited her to book clubs, cocktail evenings, and Soul Cycle classes. They wanted to be near her money, her husband's power and her multi-million-dollar townhouse on the best Georgetown Street. Women like Lauren, who only have time for those she deems worthy—i.e., those who can help her or make her look good. As for everyone else, she treats them like shit.

Now, Olivia is part of everyone *else*.

"Look, Olivia. I appreciate the initiative, okay? But there is a lot more to this than some little promotional event. There's no way you'd understand the intricacies of this, but La'Airy is facing a crisis."

"Yes, I'm aware."

"Then you understand," she says. She gives Olivia a pitying smile, like a consolation prize, then turns towards the elevators. "Well, now I really need to go."

"But that is exactly *why* you were brought in, right? To rectify the situation."

"How did you know that?"

Olivia knows what she needs to do. However sick it makes her she doesn't have a choice. *Here we go*, she thinks.

"Oh, sorry! I didn't know it was hush-hush. I think people are just excited. You have such a great reputation, and word is you are the only hope of saving the brand."

Gross. But it works. Lauren must be pleased, as she turns back towards Olivia.

"Well, that's the goal," she says nonchalantly. "But it isn't quite that simplistic. La'Airy is in a transitional phase." Olivia puts on her most amazed, *wow, you are such a role model!* face, and it seems to work. She sees it as a chance to practice, or maybe she just likes being admired, but suddenly Lauren has launched into her sales pitch. "You see, Olivia, the corporate structure is a malleable entity . . ."

She goes on, using brand lingo reinvigoration and market comprehension, while Olivia does her best impression of a star struck wannabe.

"Wow," she says. "That's fascinating."

Whoa, I had no idea it was that complicated! Olivia is far from impressed.

Olivia has seen *real spin* in her time. The kind so effortlessly invigorating, so seamlessly delivered, that you cannot help getting swept up in the excitement. You give yourself over to that bright whirlwind of promise, of new horizons, while failing to notice the cracks in that glossy foundation. And underneath, waiting, may be a dark abyss. Failure, loss, embezzled millions, coke binges with hookers and high-speed vehicles exploding in fiery bursts.

Compared to her dead ex-husband, Lauren Lugo is amateur hour. A day at the spa.

Lauren continues, using phrases like *brand harmonization* and *optic identity*, but the reality is clear.

Instead of folding or selling themselves off in pieces, La'Airy corporate has chosen a riskier path—they will *force* themselves into relevancy. Instead of going for broke, they will go for *woke*, enticing a whole new crop of shoppers. The kind with expendable income, social media accounts with millions of followers, and tastes that lean towards sparkly stripes.

That is why they chose Lauren. She understands "*millennial.*" She is one.

Lauren has been tasked with leading the overhaul, and if the spring collection is any indicator, Olivia is pretty sure what direction it will go. There will be ad campaigns featuring Gen Z'ers in glittered stripes. Maybe even some second tier "it" spokes girl, Instagram-famous, frolicking in a hip locale and dressed in sexed-up remnants of the once iconic brand. A new catchphrase, perhaps . . . *Not your grandma's La'Airy,* something like that. They will not even call it La'Airy anymore. They will rebrand it *L'Air,* keep writing checks and hope for the best.

All those years with Edwin, Olivia learned a great deal. Revamping is simply demolishing the past, then using the rubble as a base to build something shiny and new. The ones with the wrecking balls? People like Lauren Lugo.

"So yes," says Lauren, finishing her just-outside-the-elevator pitch. "It is a major task."

Enough of this. Time to nail the deal. But how?

Olivia needs to prove herself as an asset but impressing Lauren will not work. She is just a salesgirl, and a decade older at that.

Knowing valuable people is a whole other thing.

"Oh wow, what a huge job. Especially considering what you are up against! But I know you will make it happen. La'Airy is a legend, right? I mean, that's why Felix asked me to step in. He thought I could boost sales, and I had some free time, so . . ."

Please don't know Felix, thinks Olivia.

"Felix?"

Thank God.

"Harpers VP? You haven't met him?"

"Oh, I am sure I have! I meet so many people. But how do you and Felix . . ."

"Old family friend," says Olivia lightly. "We summered together on Nantucket as kids."

There it is.

Suddenly, Lauren is not so worried about the time or pressing engagements. Her interest has been piqued.

C'mon, you can make this work. You can do this, Olivia.

"Oh, I prefer the Hamptons."

"East, South or Sag Harbor?" Olivia asks lightly.

"Sag Harbor, of course! The best restaurants."

"The best."

"My friends have a lovely place a little way off from the harbor and the original Goop store. I just adore Gwyneth . . . so cutting edge. Elegant, smart. She's got it."

Olivia has never been to the Hamptons, but she knows this area is near Steven Spielberg's house. Oh, and Bill Clinton vacationed there in '88 and '89. Edwin kept mentioning the place, saying it was a fun time to buy real estate, so Olivia did a few google searches. "The prices are insane," she had said to which Edwin had shrugged. "Think of all the potential clients," he annoyingly rebutted. "It will be great for networking. A tax write-off. And besides, we are doing fine. We've got this."

A few months later, the race car crash. Then he was gone.

Lauren nods and smiles, like she has all the time in the world.

There was no meeting at corporate, obviously. No appointments to make. During their short conversation,

Olivia has gone from dismissible sales person to woman of interest, and the time has come to go in for the kill.

"Look," says Olivia, leaning in like a girlfriend ready to dish the dirt. "Ms. Lugo . . ."

"Lauren, please."

"Lauren. I cannot begin to imagine the pressure you are under with La'Airy. It must be so hard."

"I know, right? You have no idea."

"And I get it. The last thing you want to think about is some piddly event, especially here. But I promised Felix I would do my best to help with sales, and it just seemed . . . oh, well. Can't blame a girl for trying!"

Lauren tenses her jaw; she is not quite there.

"But the thing is . . . it would be a great photo op, right? Corporate would love it. Whatever happens with Harper James's placement, they would know you gave it a real, honest go. And it would not cost much, I have friends who will donate."

Lauren puts up a hand. "Enough!"

Shit.

"So," she says with a resigned sigh. "What kind of budget are we talking about?"

***

Moments later, Olivia bounces back on the La'Airy sales floor, elated. It is nothing, really. Just a little gathering. It will not save the world, or La'Airy for that matter. But it's a start.

Still, Olivia has not felt prouder in . . . she cannot remember the last time. This is what it feels like to accomplish something real. Not a fundraiser centerpiece, or the hardest level spin class. Not a dinner party for people you can barely stand. Something you had to fight for, and then won.

"Well now."

Olivia looks up, grinning ear to ear. Marguerite is staring at her, a faint smile playing on her lips. "A lady never gloats, and besides, we haven't the time. Planning an event takes effort if I remember correctly. It has been *years*."

Olivia nods, giddily. "I'll get a notebook. We can jot down some ideas! I mean, after we put out the new collection."

"New collection? Please. I have no intention of doing such a thing. Besides, we have a party to plan." That is when something unexpected happens—a sound Olivia has not yet heard.

Marguerite laughing, loud and bright. In that moment, as it echoes across the empty department, she looks a quarter her age. Like a teenager, full of life and ready to take on the world.

"You are full of surprises, Olivia," she says. "I'll give you that."

She laughs some more, then sighs. "Well, why not? A little La'Airy tete-a-tete. A final lark." She gazes out across the deserted and seemingly depressed La'Airy floor. "At the very least, it will fill the time. We haven't much else to do around here, have we?" Olivia grins from ear-to-ear. "Let's do this." she says.

Chapter Ten

Hope Springs Eternal

A week and a half after meeting the infamous Lauren Lugo, and achieving the impossible go ahead, Olivia and Marguerite stand at the entrance of a tucked-away third floor lounge contemplating the fruits of their effort. The event will begin in just under two hours.

The previous days have been a blur, the nights sleepless, Olivia existing in an alternate reality of lists and phone calls, exasperated responses, and strategic coercion. Now, Olivia stands quietly, nervous energy coursing through her veins, as she awaits the verdict that matters most.

The night she met Lauren, Olivia had been full of confident adrenaline, triumphant at the yes. Only the next morning, in the light of day, had the reality of the situation taken hold, starting with an unexpected visit.

Felix.

He had arrived moments after opening, resplendent as always in his perfectly cut suit. After a brief hello, he went silent for a moment, contemplating Marguerite and Olivia from across the La'Airy counter. "I had a rather fascinating call from corporate," he said. "Regarding a promotional event." He focused on Olivia, his smooth face unreadable. *How did he do that,* Olivia had wondered. *Note to self, get the name of Felix's Botox person.*

"I take it this is all of you're doing," he told her.

"Well, that's true, in a manner of speaking," stuttered Olivia, suddenly overwhelmed with guilt. She felt like a high school student who'd gotten caught skipping fourth period, or even worse, smoking behind the bleachers. "I know it is unexpected, and perhaps a reach, I mean, I haven't worked here long, I know, but I saw an opportunity and . . ."

Felix stopped her with a raised hand. Then he did something completely unexpected.

He laughed. More of a chuckle, really, but the sound was undeniable amusement.

"Well," he said. "La'Airy corporate has informed me they would be more than happy to sponsor a trunk show," he said, then turned to Marguerite, eyebrows barely raised. She smiled and gave a little shrug. "I'm as surprised as you, Felix. Though, I must admit, I am impressed with Olivia's initiative. Change is inevitable, I suppose, but we mustn't forget what truly matters. And after all these years, you, Felix . . . still have an eye for talent."

The two exchange smiles, and Olivia knows they are speaking of something much larger than her. A shared legacy, the intimacy of time and experience. Still, she cannot help but feel validated.

"So," said Felix, dropping the smile, once again transforming into his cool, elegant managerial voice. "As there has not been a La'Airy event for quite a while, and the request is rather sudden, there are some, how best to put this? Stipulations. Restraints, perhaps that is a better word. So best we make some decisions immediately."

Olivia was already reaching for a notebook.

Restraints was the perfect word. While Felix assured Olivia and Marguerite that Harper James was supportive of the endeavor—though Olivia caught a flash of hesitation in his eyes during the pronouncement—the time frame and locale were an issue. "We have a full roster," he informed them, "but I was able to do some juggling of the schedule and confirm a date."

A week and a half. Even worse, the only available space would be the cramped third floor lounge that, in recent years, was better known as a storage space. "We will have it thoroughly cleaned and the floors polished. I've already contacted maintenance about a fresh coat of paint. But then there is the issue of budget."

In other words, there wasn't one. Five thousand, that's what Olivia quoted to Lauren, even then believing it to be a stretch. And now it was cut in half.

"Ultimately, there are only the basics available to you," Felix had concluded, and Olivia silently agreed. "A storage room, seven days, little funding and a general lack of Harper James support. So, with that in mind, is this an endeavor you would still like to pursue?"

Olivia didn't need to speak; the answer was all over her face.

Hell, yeah!

For the first time since leaving D.C., Olivia had a goal beyond just surviving. And considering what she survived—the loss of her husband, reputation, net worth and entire community—how hard could it be to plan a little event? A cinch compared to what she was used to in D.C.

She had no idea what was to come. Luckily, she had a secret weapon.

***

For the past week, Marguerite has transformed before Olivia's eyes. Always energetic, she has gone into overdrive, throwing herself into preparations. While time on the La'Airy sales floor was filled with meaningless time fillers in lieu of customers, the previous days were a blur of activity. Olivia watched as Marguerite manned the phone, calling in favors. A caterer she had known forever, a paper store on the Upper East Side for stationery. Each conversation following the same script. Every word strategically selected.

First, the greeting. "Hello, darling. Yes, it has been . . . forever, indeed . . ."

Next, the catch-up, i.e., discussion regarding physical ailments and the general difficulties intrinsic to aging, followed by the mentioning of shared associates, followed by discussion of the physical ailments and general aging difficulties as they pertain to the aforementioned associates.

"Your arthritis? What a shame. Have you seen a specialist? Well, it isn't pretty, getting older. Did you hear about Mark Rothstein's triple bypass?"

On to reminiscing about the good old days.

"She was a lark, oh yes. And husband number four, which was that? The oil baron, of course. That gown for the Black and White Ball, remember that? Dior, I think. Lovely. But you must wear the clothes, isn't that true? You cannot allow them to wear you. A good tailor is paramount!"

Finally, the pitch. "I know you are retired, my love, but something has come up and, well, I cannot begin to imagine hiring some inexperienced young thing for such an occasion. I need good taste for this event, just like we used to do."

Then Marguerite would go into lavish specifics, citing the chef's mushroom caps from a 1962 mixer, or the delightful cream cardstock of invites from a 1981 trunk show.

Ultimately, the spiel.

"I am in desperate need of your artistry, darling. I don't have much funding, but I thought perhaps for old time's sake . . ."

Olivia had watched, marveling, as Marguerite charmed and praised and leaned back her head to laugh, a musical trill that filled the floor. She seemed to age backwards before Olivia's eyes.

A warm goodbye, Marguerite would hang up the phone and turn to Olivia with a smile.

It worked every time.

As for Olivia, the idea had been hers, but she knew her role: foot soldier. It was she who ran uptown to fetch the invitations, and who brought back the daily progress report of the venue. "The room has been cleared," Olivia would report. "The wood floor has been polished, and they've just started painting the walls."

"Go back, won't you dear? Take a little picture with your fancy phone."

"Oh no," Marguerite would say once she returned, eyes narrowed as she confronted the image of a wall swiped with color. "What would you call that color?"

"Taupe?"

"I would call it muck. It will not do, and it isn't the La'Airy color way. See to fixing it, will you? And what are . . . those monstrosities?" She asked, pointing to stacks of plastic chairs and a folded card table.

"The furnishings, I suppose. Maintenance brought them up yesterday."

"Those are not furnishings. They are horrible and tacky plastic chairs and a picnic table. Please sort that out as well, will you, Olivia?"

Olivia threw herself into each task, feeling her confidence renewed. It was just like old times, when she had been the one to secure sponsors for the *WTC*'s charity balls or see to the menus at their various fundraisers. Only those jobs, a one-time means of proving herself, had soon grown into annoyances. *All that effort for what final purpose?* is what Olivia always thought.

This time it felt different.

It was Olivia who negotiated with the annoyed painting crew, insisting there was no need to check with management over such a minor change of plans. "Felix has given me full responsibility to oversee the process!" She'd insisted. "Don't worry about the inventory, either. In fact, why don't I just run to the paint store myself? You guys can take a little break. How many, what do you call them—cans, right? How many of those do we need?"

Days were spent rushing through the hallways of La'Airy, racing out to catch cabs and returning with arms full of boxed invitations, silver platters borrowed from an elderly woman on Central Park East and white cotton tablecloths. For the first time, Olivia felt thankful for her invisibility in the Harper James spectrum. Eyes shifted upon her arrival, other employees turning away with suddenly discovered tasks. Only one person seemed to note her activities.

She'd been lugging several white plastic bags—hidden inside, the covert cans of pale salmon colored paint, a shade deemed La'Airy appropriate by Marguerite—when a voice had stopped her.

"Well now, you've been busy, haven't you?"

Olivia had looked up to see the elderly man who headed up security. They had only met briefly once or twice when his rounds had taken him by La'Airy. Marguerite had lit up upon his arrival, and the two had chatted briefly. Marguerite had introduced him as Willard, informing Olivia he'd been around Harper James almost as long as she had.

"Longer, maybe," he had said. But then again, "I don't make quite the same impression as this gorgeous looker!"

Olivia had watched, shocked, as Marguerite blushed. "Charming man," she had said, as they watched him walk away in his crisp white shirt, security badge gleaming on his chest. "They've been trying to get him to retire, but he refuses. Good for him, that's what I say. And his son, what a brilliant young man. A tech genius. Works in security as well. Heads it up, tell you the truth."

It was Willard who had helped Olivia carry the bags upstairs, never commenting on what might be the heavy contents. "Well, now. You've created quite the stir at Harper James, haven't you?" He said, eyes glimmering.

"I have?" She said, thinking about the diverted eyes, the employees who seemed to go out of their way just attempting to avoid her. "Everyone seems to make an extra effort to avoid me."

"Exactly," he responded, offering no explanation. Perhaps it is the kindness in his eyes, but for the first time that week, Olivia allowed herself to feel the weight of expectation. She realizes how nervous she was; how fearful she was that this will end in failure.

"I just want this event to go well." she said.

But what if it doesn't? The thought came suddenly, crushing down on her like a lead weight. What if, despite all the effort, Olivia just crashed and burned?

Still, she wanted this to succeed. She can't remember wanting something this bad in a long time. Not even a Chanel 2.55.

Chapter Eleven

White Knuckled

Thirty minutes to go. Olivia and Marguerite survey their work, and for the first time that day, Marguerite has gone silent. Olivia applies her city rose pink lipstick—the perfect shade for an *afternoon shopping event.* Lips pursed, she scans the room with a fierce and critical eye.

The past few hours have been a frenzy of final preparations. Marguerite is like a four-star fashion general in charge. She hurried about, dictating orders at a rapid speed, while never seeming to lose her cool. "Fetch a steamer, please?" She had said, pointing out wrinkles in the cream tablecloth. "And do you see the white lilies in the flower arrangement? They are wilted!" Olivia couldn't see any wrinkles, and there were only a few hidden lilies, but she'd jumped at every request. "Why don't we just remove them?"

Olivia had followed Marguerite to the rack at the center of the room, full, with classic La'Airy staples—elegant dresses, silk blouses, blazers. As for the new collection, it was there too, only hidden in a corner of the room and obscured by potted, tall plants.

"This won't do, not at all." she had said, moving a hanger to the left. "Do you see the difference, my dear? The spacing is completely off. It must be precise, exact. We reviewed this important detail once before. It's the *La'Airy way.*"

The *La'Airy way* required a rewashing of all the coffee and teacups, even though they sparkled, and the finger sandwiches—cut in perfect, uber skinny rectangles to mimic the La'Airy stripe logo—needed to be rearranged. "Darling Olivia, please make sure the sandwiches are in good order, and divided by type: egg salad, chicken, and cucumber. And then in alphabetical order; chicken, cucumber and then egg."

The dividing sheers in the makeshift dressing rooms were too sheer, so Olivia had fetched replacements; the lighting too harsh, so Olivia had tracked down a maintenance man to replace all the fluorescent bulbs with a more flattering wattage. Olivia had run and chased for last minute must haves, her nervousness growing with each passing minute, while Marguerite appeared unphased. In fact, she looked great. Her eyes gleamed as she circled the room with confident steps, her cheeks flushed a fetching pink. She looked ten years younger, calmly dictating commands, as Olivia was the polar opposite. Frazzled, to put it mildly.

Now that they were finally ready, Marguerite had gone silent. Next to her, Olivia sucks in her breath, waiting for the final word.

"Well," she finally says. "I suppose this will do."

"Now you . . . are . . . how to put this? A bit manic." Olivia almost laughs. "Maybe a quick touch-up?" She reaches out and pats Olivia's hand. "There's nothing to worry about, you'll see. Everything will go splendidly." She checks her watch. "Quickly go down to cosmetics where they will touch you up . . . you could use some more color to your face and another coat of mascara. Maybe Mimi at Chanel is available. Then hurry back. The guests will be here at any moment."

The event is scheduled for three o'clock. It is ten past. Olivia has redone her French twist, applied a swipe of blusher and, of course, an extra swipe of the shade of city rose pink lipstick. She has taken several deep breaths—inhale through the nose, out through the mouth—like they taught in that zen sweat class she once took. *Time to meditate and focus from within,* the teacher had shouted. *Give me ten mindful crunches, people! Right now! And keep hold of your zen!*

While she may look put together, inside Olivia is growing more frantic by the second.

Seconds seem like hours. Olivia fidgets and straightens the racks, again. She paces to the food table for a last minute check. Olivia has a deja vu . . . *feels just like that horrible night,* though this time her own financial future and well-being are on the line. She takes deep breaths. They should be here by now. *Someone* should be here by now. *Anyone! Oh God.* Olivia thinks.

At the refreshment table, Lauren, who had just arrived, gives a long sigh. She checks her phone for the fifteenth time since she has arrived. It has only been ten minutes, but her transformation has been extraordinary. When she showed up at 3 p.m., she was all smiles. "Oh wow," she had said, looking around the room with wide eyes. "This place looks amazing! How did you pull this off on your budget? Seriously, Olivia, I'm impressed."

"It was all Marguerite!" Olivia had said, which Lauren ignored. "How cute are these sandwiches," she'd gushed instead, helping herself to them. She seemed so pleased, she didn't even realize the new delivery of clothing was noticeably absent, i.e., tucked behind artificial fiddle leaf fig trees in the corner.

As for Marguerite, she was equally as dismissive. After a cursory hello, she made herself busy, wiping invisible lint off garments and straightening perfectly aligned chairs. Olivia was left to entertain Lauren, which had worked well—for a short while.

3:15, and she is officially antsy. She texts and sighs, no longer bothering with pleasant conversation. In fact, she has gone completely silent, other than to pipe up with the occasional barked questions. "The time was three, right?"

"Yes, Lauren. 3:00."

"Did the guests know the right location?"

"Yes, Lauren. They did. We even gave them directions. Third floor, left corridor."

"Well, maybe they got lost," she interrupts, not bothering to hide the sarcasm.

"You know, most people arrive on time for trunk shows," she says, not bothering to look up from her phone. "You sent out the invites, right Olivia?"

"Of course!" says Olivia, though she hadn't. "And, in plenty of time!" While Olivia had run countless errands, when it came to the guest list, Marguerite had insisted she would take the lead. Olivia had been concerned, especially after the Rolodex fiasco. "You said there wasn't anyone to invite," she had reminded Marguerite. "That they were all married or relocated. Or dead."

"I wasn't looking that hard," Marguerite had said, waving her hand dismissively. "I can call in some favors, darling. Don't give it a second thought."

Now, it is Olivia's *only* thought.

"Well, I can't wait all day," says Lauren.

"I'm sure they'll be here at any moment!" says Olivia.

Lauren simply grunts and continues texting.

Olivia quietly speed walks over to Marguerite, who hums to herself while rearranging the already perfectly arranged flowers. "Where is everyone?" she whispers. "I'm worried."

"Worry will get you nothing but wrinkles."

"But what if no one shows up!"

"Oh, they will. I'm sure of it."

Olivia wants to believe her, but with each passing second—and sigh—the reality weighs heavier on her shoulders. *Why did she leave Marguerite to handle the guest list?* All this time, she's been racing around, running meaningless errands. Lugging cans of paint, discussing stripe-shaped finger sandwiches, trying to find a cloth napkin in Marguerite's preferred shade of white. "This is more eggshell than ivory, so it won't work. Everything just has to be perfect!" All the while overlooking the most important aspect of the entire event.

The goddamn guests.

At 3:28, Lauren reaches her breaking point. She stands suddenly, reaches for her purse and glares at Olivia. "You know, I really went out of my way to make this happen."

"I know!" says Olivia. "It means so much to me! To . . . us!"

"I figured, give the woman a chance. Let her try to prove herself. You seemed so determined, Olivia. But to say I'm disappointed, well . . . that's an understatement."

"I'm sure they'll be here any . . ."

"3:30!" says Lauren, holding up her phone. "Are you telling me that every single guest is thirty minutes late?" She shakes her head. "I went out on a limb, Olivia. Told corporate it was worth the effort. Not worth the effort, this branch of La'Airy! That's what they said. A lost cause, they told me."

Olivia feels her stomach clench, her anger rising. She glances across the room, where Marguerite is still turned from them. *Not worth the effort?* She thinks. So, maybe the event hadn't worked out, but Marguerite had given decades to this brand. How dare she be so disrespectful?

"But I convinced them, Olivia. I figured if you pulled this off, maybe we could find another home for you with the La'Airy family. Turns out I was wrong. I should have known better, considering your . . . mentor."

"Hold on," Olivia says, feeling her anger bubble up like red hot Hawaiian lava. "Marguerite is a wonderful leader. She's taught me so much. You have no idea. She knows this brand inside and out. She's the best advocate for . . ."

"Oh yeah? Then where is everyone?" She turns. "Marguerite, if you're so good at this, maybe you're the one in the know. We've got the room, the appetizers, the flowers. Now where, exactly, are the clients?"

They both look at Marguerite, back still turned. For a moment, no one speaks. Beyond the muffled Fifth Avenue traffic, the dinging of a far-off elevator—utter silence. Marguerite drops her hands from the flowers and lifts her chin. Then, with painful slowness, she turns around. Olivia braces for her pained expression.

She is smiling.

"The guests? Oh, I believe they've just arrived."

Lauren shakes her head. "And how exactly . . ."

"Excellent hearing, Lauren. You develop that when you actually make an effort to listen to people."

That's when Olivia hears something, too. Clacking down the marble-tiled hall. Growing closer, until . . .

"Marguerite, darling!" There in the doorway, an elegant mirage—pearls, cocktail suit, nude stockings and kitten heels. She might have been sixty, or ninety or anywhere between—she has that indeterminate age that can only be achieved via years of self-maintenance and some magician practicing on the Upper East Side. Her stole is a fox—like the kind with a head—and the matching Halston-esque pillbox hat sits perkily on her head. Beneath, winged eyeliner, frosted pale pink lips and cheekbones that have been carefully contoured by the artistry of a master.

It is as though a glamorous apparition has manifested before them, circa 1952.

Before Olivia can close her gaping mouth, the woman is striding towards them in a mist of Chanel Number 5. "Darling!" she says to Marguerite, air kisses fly, and the two stand there with gripped hands, staring with excitement at one another. "It has been far too long!"

"Mrs. Lowen," says Marguerite. "It was so very kind of you to . . ."

"Dodie!" the woman shrieks. "Call me Dodie! How many times must I ask?" She turns to Olivia. "Decades!" she whispers. "That's how long! Well, at least one face lift ago." She stops suddenly, eyes narrowing. "And you must be Olivia."

"How did you . . ."

"Oh, please. I know everything. And perhaps a little birdie was chirping as well." Before Olivia can think to respond, she has turned her back to Marguerite. "You're right, she is charming! Such a stylish little girl."

The woman steps back, smiles and removes her stole. "Now, have we begun yet? Or am I the first to arrive? Where is the champagne?"

"You're the only one to arrive thus far," says a voice. Mrs. Lowen, Marguerite and Olivia turn to the voice—Lauren, phone still in hand, looking even more dour than before. "Seems this will be a party of one," said Lauren.

"Well, that can't be true. Where are the others?"

Lauren forces a smile. "I'm afraid there aren't any others."

"You must be mistaken," Mrs. Lowen tells her, voice dripping with the kind of warmth that disguises a block of ice.

In the distance, a faint ding.

"I'm afraid so," says Lauren, annoyance oozing from beneath her plastic smile. Unlike Olivia, she is not mesmerized by this woman. "Unfortunately, Mrs. Lowen—Dodie—you are the only invitee who has actually shown."

Mrs. Lowen widens her eyes—though her forehead is incapable of wrinkling, she is obviously perplexed. "No, that cannot be," she says. Then she stops suddenly, steps forward and dramatically raises a gloved finger. "Ah, there they are! I hear them coming now."

In silence, everyone turns to the door. As if on cue, the clacking of heels, the voices beginning to rise. A cacophony of high-pitched laughter as they make their way, the chirpy enthusiastic pack, from the elevator. Make their way down the long hallway, voices growing louder with each step, until . . .

Next to Olivia, Marguerite smiles.

"Ms. Lowen has excellent hearing as well."

"I haven't seen you since that Palm Beach gala, oh . . . when was that? 1980, wasn't it? I remember because that Beatle was there, you know the one, with the long black hair. And glasses, too, I think. Could it really be that long ago?"

Another voice shrieks, "Great Granny, try that on for size. Yes, she finally agreed to debut, but I worry . . . one of those millennials, you know? A diamond nose stud. That's her idea of refinement."

And another, "Ages since I came to New York! A show, perhaps. Tell me, how does one get tickets for that Hamilton brouhaha? I hear it's the latest and best!" Or, "is there something trendier I should know about?"

Olivia watches, amazed, as the women drink champagne and circulate, voices overlapping in many enthusiastic conversations at once.

It has only been a few minutes since they arrived, bursting through the door as a boisterous, elegant pack, and Olivia is standing in the same place, still in shock. More unexpected than the turn-out, even, is those who actually turned out. Olivia has been to events like this before—in her former life, trunk shows were how you filled time between aerial yoga and charity gala planning committees—but she has never seen a group like this. At those events, dress would run the gamut from Lulu Lemon ("just ran over from Pilates!") to Prada ("this old thing?"). But no one, not even the highest rank of socialite, ever put in this kind of effort.

And there are a lot of them—two dozen women, maybe more, and their ages are more Florida snowbird than Hampton's summer house share. Senior citizens, but not the ordinary kind—these are the La Goulue ladies who lunch in their full, glorious regalia.

In other words, they are utterly stunning.

Olivia watches as Marguerite is swept from woman to woman, group to group—everyone wants a moment of her time. They fawn at her with praise and reminiscence, tell her it has been too long . . . and actually mean it. "Of course, I came!" Says one. "What's a few hundred miles for you, Marguerite?"

They have come from everywhere, Olivia realizes, traveling by Amtrak, private driver, private jet. They have all come for one sole reason—Marguerite, who catches Olivia's eye at that very moment, shooting

Olivia a visual and unspoken message, as if to say, *meet me over there, in the corner, Olivia,* without ever breaking conversation. "Now, just give me one moment to direct my young acolyte. Yes, the one I told you about, Olivia. I'll be back in two snaps to show you my favorite picks of the collection, Mrs. Rothschild! There's a dress that is so you!"

Mrs. Rothschild? As in, *Rothschild* Rothschild? And why do these women know *her* name?

Olivia heads to the corner, still in a state of shock, where Marguerite is already waiting.

"Might you explain, my dear, the reason you are standing in one place like a deer in the headlights?" she says, voice low. "The point was to move merchandise, was it not?"

"Of course! I was just . . . I guess I'm a little shocked. I mean, I never expected so many people, or that . . ."

"I simply called in a few favors," she says with a tiny smile. "Must impress the corporate office, mustn't we, just as requested. That is what Lauren expected, was it not?"

"This was the last thing Lauren expected," says Olivia.

For a moment, they both gaze at their higher-up, who stands off to the side looking deeply uncomfortable.

Possibly insecure even. Lauren is so overwhelmed by the scene before her, she makes no attempt to join in or even look busy—she just stares, phone hanging limply by her side, unsure of her next move. A fierce corporate up-and-comer in designer suits and an impeccable and fresh blow-out (maybe she went to the Blo Dry Bar on E. 57th & Lexington?) —but in this crowd, she looks like a withered, out-of-place nobody without a glamourous bone in her body.

"Oh, she's just taken aback, I suppose," says Marguerite. "Here she was, thinking this was a dud. That no one would show."

"Wait a minute," says Olivia with a sudden realization. "They all came at the same time. Not three, but . . . wait. You told them later, right? Just to mess with Lauren?"

"I simply believe in the power of a grand entrance. Now, if I *really* wanted to—how did you put it? 'Mess with Lauren' . . . well, there are far more effective methods. Like selling inordinate amounts of merchandise, for example."

Olivia nods, and for a moment, they simply smile at each other.

"Go on, then," says Marguerite. "They already know all about you. And they're waiting."

The next two hours are a furious flurry of activity. Olivia is in hot demand, called to from across the room, beckoned mid-conversation, pulled from woman to woman. They want her opinion—*does the salmon make me look sallow? I like the slim pencil silhouette, but tell me honestly, is it a tad too revealing? I'm just not sure how this blouse should button, and I can't see. Have I misbuttoned it? Oh my goodness . . . I must have left my readers in the car!*

To each guest, Olivia offers her full attention and honest opinions. She runs from client to client, making suggestions and pairing pieces into ensembles; she demonstrates possibilities in front of the tri-fold mirror. "Just take this in a bit, lift here and—isn't that lovely?"

She is greeted again and again by smiles and compliments. "You are a dream," the women tell her. "Just as Marguerite said! You remind me of her back in the day. That eye is a gift, Olivia, darling. Don't ever forget it."

Clothing is pulled from the rack, the dressing room line is too long—at some point, Olivia pulls off the curtain and pins it from wall to wall, constructing a larger makeshift dressing room.

"Aren't you ingenious, darling!" The women say, then disappear behind their giggles. Their gossip carries over.

At some point, more merchandise is needed. "You must have this in another color?" a woman with a masterful bouffant hairdo and even bigger diamond ring says. "Not here," Olivia says. "But upstairs. Perhaps I could run upstairs."

"Oh, please don't go!" says another woman on the right, patiently waiting her turn. "I need your help!"

"So do I!" says the woman to her left. "You haven't seen the cocktail dress on me yet!"

Olivia looks helplessly at Marguerite, who is equally as busy across the room, demonstrating the various modes of wearing a blazer to a small circle of adoring shoppers.

"What about her?" Booms a voice, and everyone turns to see Mrs. Rothschild, still-gloved finger pointing straight at Lauren. "You work for La'Airy?"

"Well, yes," says Lauren. "But I'm in the corporate office, I'm a La'Airy executive and not a Harper James employee, so therefore I don't . . ."

"Good, then you know the backstock. Go upstairs and fetch more, will you, darling? I'd like to see more separates . . . more suiting. You know, I have a few business lunches to attend soon."

A moment passes as Lauren opens her mouth and closes it. Finally, she nods and heads towards the door. "Oh, and darling?" Says Mrs. Rothschild. Lauren turns.

"Make sure it is the good stuff, will you? None of those monstrosities like behind the potted plant."

At some point, as Olivia is in the middle of ringing up purchases . . . how long have they been at this? Olivia finally glances at her watch and is shocked that the two hours are almost up. She gets the strange feeling that she is being watched.

A quick glance up and a confirmation—amidst the rush of bodies and boisterous goodbyes and retrieval of coats and gathering of Harper James bags full of brand-new purchases, one still and lithe figure by the door appears. A tall man, standing very still, watching Olivia with great interest.

Felix.

He catches her eye and nods. At his lips, a faint smile.

By 5:30, all the women are gone. All that remains are Olivia and Marguerite, who are going over their event sales numbers, and Lauren, who is talking Felix's ear off.

"You wouldn't believe the crap those ad firms threw at us!" she says, then giggles. "I mean, you rebrand into something better, right? That's the whole point! But those guys didn't understand the first thing about this new and contemporary La'Airy direction."

Felix nods, listening intently, though his face is un-readable. As for Lauren, hers is obvious—utter adoration. She has been covertly drinking ever since the stock room walk-of-shame, but not covertly enough for Olivia to miss it. She had been pretending to tidy the refreshment area, while secretly combining the final dregs of four champagne bottles together, when she finally noticed Felix . . . still standing there, unobtrusive and calm, in his elegant suit.

Forget the incognito act. He had been found out, and for the last twenty minutes, he has had a tipsy Lauren babbling like crazy. Whether she wants to impress him, or fuck him, you can't be sure—at this point, Olivia has no idea. Whatever it may be, it is embarrassing. And somehow, strangely entertaining.

"Poor man," says Marguerite. She sits next to Olivia, calculator in hand, doing a final tabulation of that day's purchases.

"Why isn't he running away?"

"Perhaps he wants to congratulate us, my dear. As well he should."

Marguerite sets the calculator aside, sighs and stands. "Well, I believe we are done here," she says with enough finality that Lauren shockingly shuts up and turns. "Oh, yes?" says Felix, taking the moment to step towards them. "And was the event as successful as it appeared?"

"Well, we barely made a dent in the new stock," says Marguerite.

"Because no one could see it!" pipes up Lauren. "I mean, you put it behind . . ."

". . . As I was saying, we did just fine," says Marguerite, ignoring her. She holds up her clipboard to Felix. "Take a look."

Felix takes the clipboard and scans it, then nods.

"Quite well indeed. Impressive, ladies."

"Eighteen thousand dollars in two hours," says Marguerite. "Perhaps the most successful event in La'Airy history." She smiles at Lauren. "Even without the new merchandise, we did well."

"Hold up," says Lauren, reaching for the clipboard. "Let me see. There is no way. I need to make sure that figure is correct. Corporate will want to know."

"Yes, corporate will want to know all about this," says Felix. "They will be pleased, I believe."

Lauren goes silent.

"Surprising, this kind of success. Especially considering the recent department reviews I've received from your higher-ups," says Felix.

"You read those?" says Lauren, looking shocked.

"Of course," says Felix. "I keep abreast of all Harper James happenings. I read every single one. It's surprising, this success, considering the rather dour projections in your reports. Has there been a miscommunication?"

Lauren bristles. She sucks in her breath and stands up straight, jaw clenched tight. The buzz has worn off, Olivia can tell.

"No, those were accurate. This event, while successful, was an obvious anomaly. Nothing has changed. Everything will proceed as expected."

Felix nods. "I thought as much," he says, then turns to Marguerite. "But quite the triumph, was it not, Marguerite? Quite a way to end a successful run."

End? Thinks Olivia. *What does that . . .*

"And I do look forward to your retirement party," says Felix. What a gift you've been to the Harper James community!"

"Retirement party?" says Olivia, no longer able to hold it back. "Are you retiring, Marguerite?"

Marguerite gives her a sad smile. "Yes, my dear." She reaches out and pats her hand. "It has been a long time coming, truth be told. I am exhausted, and there are other adventures to be had. And when the news came last week, well, between you and me . . . it was

223

bittersweet. All good things, as they say, and that includes La'Airy."

"Not La'Airy," barks Lauren. "Just the Harper James partnership."

"Wait, I don't . . . La'Airy is closing?"

Marguerite nods. "It was only made official last week. I had planned on telling you but felt it better to wait until after the event. And if anything, this proved what I already knew. La'Airy may be over, but you are just beginning in this industry."

"La'Airy is not closing," says Lauren, her voice now a hiss. "Look, Olivia," she says, throwing a glare towards Marguerite. "One thing is true. You do have a future in retail. That is why I showed up today, even though . . . that is why I stayed as well. I have spoken with corporate about you, and they trust my instinct. I think we can find another role for you in the company—not at Harper James, obviously, but one with better growth potential." She leans in and smiles, her face dripping with a faux authenticity Olivia knows well. She has seen it many times before in her former life. Mothers at school, women in the league, wives at various cocktail parties and society gatherings—all smiling at her with the rapt attention you give someone who matters. Someone whose husband, and status, matter.

Those same women who disappeared as quickly as a flash sample sale.

"There is always room for new talent at La'Airy," she says. "And we want to keep you in the La'Airy family."

"That's an interesting offer," says Felix. "And you should keep your options open, Olivia. In fact, Marguerite and I were discussing this very topic. We believe there are opportunities for you at Harper James as well. Immediate ones."

Olivia is shocked and thrilled and conflicted in the same moment. She looks at Marguerite, who is calmly gathering her supplies. Reaching for her pen, her calculator, the clipboard. Her hands are long, elegant, carefully manicured. For the first time, Olivia notes the marks, so faint you'd have to search for them. *Hyperpigmentation,* she thinks. *If only she had used sunblock on her hands! A few IPL treatments could fix that . . .*

The La'Airy family. The words ring in her ears. Marguerite was part of the La'Airy family before Lauren even came into existence. She gave her life to that family, and just like that, they return the favor by pushing her out into the cold. So typical it seems. She showed so much loyalty. And in return, they really could not give a rat's ass.

"You know, Felix," says Olivia. "I'd really love to hear more. I mean can you give a hint at least?" Olivia is so pumped on adrenaline from the success of the selling event that she can't contain herself from pushing Felix for details. "Olivia, my dear, I can't disclose anything at this very moment, but I do believe timing is everything, and yours is perfect. We will go over the entirety tomorrow morning just after the store morning huddle."

For once my timing is right! thinks Olivia. She says goodbye to Marguerite and heads towards the elevator. Dead in her tracks is Lauren Lugo. "Oh, hi Lauren. I'm just on my way out, though while I have you here, let me just say I wouldn't work for you or with you, or whatever for all the coffee at Starbucks. La'Airy is so iconic and you are just the opposite. I appreciate your offer though I am formally not accepting it. Good luck, Lauren. I think you're gonna need it."

Olivia steps into the elevator, hits the L button, and watches Lauren's look of surprise as the elevator doors slowly close. She smiles and can feel her face flush with excitement. *Ding!* The doors open once again, and this time, Olivia steps out with a newborn confidence she hasn't felt in years. Olivia grabs her cell and makes a call. "Mom! I'm just getting off work and heading to the train. I may have some cool news to share . . . I will know more tomorrow after a meeting with Felix, but he told me there are immediate opportunities at Harper James! I'm not exactly sure what's going on but I think it could be important." Gladys squeals, "Oh honey!! That's wonderful! I can't wait for the news myself . . . now, get home soon. The brisket is in the oven . . ."

About the Author

Toni Glickman is a former retail executive, who spent twenty years in the cashmere and silk-studded front lines in the luxury space of this piranha infested industry. Toni, in her provocative new book *Bitches of Fifth Avenue,* reveals the story of life behind the luxury lines—what the client never sees. The exhaustion, depression, and anxiety-ridden days of an employee's experience, which clients never realize. The fear of low sales numbers, of losing rank, of losing a job to someone with a better client book. Also, there's the fear of returned merchandise and the constant worry of losing a client to another salesperson. Never a moment of purity, or peace, or calm. It is a life lived constantly on the edge. *Saks Fifth Avenue*, *Prada*, *Jil Sander*, *Chanel*, *Bloomingdale's* and *Burberry*—these were just a few brands in which Toni achieved success before ultimately being backstabbed by those she thought she could trust.

Moving up the ladder from sales associate to industry executive, Toni Glickman compares working in the field to the front lines of a minefield. Her colleagues exemplified the mines in which she had to navigate through in order to survive and make her sales numbers, which is all that matters at the end of the day when the cash registers close. An employee in this industry is only respected by how much business is done, in business lingo: "day over day, month over month, and year over year." Expectations run high, illness is not permitted, and personal lives are ignored. It is report after report, endless conference calls, sales strategies, and goals. Personal shoppers do whatever it takes—it is sell, sell, sell.

Toni Glickman now enjoys life as a real estate professional, where she sets her own schedule and no longer needs to contend with maneuvering "bitchy" retail colleagues. She's also a Francophile, plays classical piano, loves the cinema, travel, her children, family, friends, and Teacup Pomeranian, Madonna.

Upcoming New Release

TONI GLICKMAN'S

BITCHES OF FIFTH AVENUE
CUTTHROAT COUTURE
BOOK TWO

The "team' of personal shoppers inside the Salon are anything but welcoming, particularly the lead stylist, Zoe. Olivia tries to get the lay of the land as she shadows anyone in the Salon who is kind enough to help her. But she hardly knows where the light switch is, let alone who is who…

Olivia takes particular note of the other shoppers . . . the people who now surround Olivia, the Bitches of Fifth Avenue . . .

**For more information
visit:** www.SpeakingVolumes.us

Upcoming New Release

LISA SHERMAN'S

FORGET ME NOT
FORGET ME
BOOK ONE

**How can you know who you really are
if you can't remember your past?**

Wanda Dellas is living someone else's life: that's the sense she's had since a mysterious accident five years earlier...

Barely scraping by, Wanda cleans offices at night in order to support her young daughter. She tells herself that anyone would believe they're meant for a different existence. Yet she can't shake the sense that she's missing something...

**For more information
visit:** www.SpeakingVolumes.us

Upcoming New Release

BRIAN FELGOISE
DAVID TABATSKY

FILTHY RICH LAWYERS
THE EDUCATION OF RYAN COLEMAN
BOOK ONE

Inspired by real-life class-action lawyers, *The Education of Ryan Coleman* begins in a Texas courtroom, where an ambitious attorney from Philadelphia chases his share of a lawsuit and gets his ass reamed by the judge. During this "trial-by-fire," Coleman meets Eugenia Cauley, a female legal shark whose life ends tragically…

"The lightning paced humor provides a serious message about corruption in class action litigation. This is a hilarious satire about a very real problem." —Matt Flynn, author, *Milwaukee Jihad*

For more information
visit: www.SpeakingVolumes.us

Printed in Great Britain
by Amazon